National and international bestselling author **Joya Ryan** is the author of the Shattered series, which includes *Break Me Slowly*, *Possess Me Slowly*, and *Capture Me Slowly*. She has also written the Sweet Torment series, which includes *Breathe You In* and *Only You*. Passionate about both cooking and dancing (despite not being too skilled at the latter), she loves spending time at home. Along with her husband and her two sons, she resides in California.

Visit Joya Ryan online:
www.joyaryan.com
www.twitter.com/joyaryanauthor

T0349958

By Joya Ryan

Yours Tonight
Yours Completely
Yours Forever

Yours
Forever

JOYA RYAN

piatkus

PIATKUS

First published in the US in 2015
First published in Great Britain in 2015 by Piatkus

3 5 7 9 10 8 6 4 2

A CIP catalogue record for this book
is available from the British Library.

ISBN 978-0-349-40721-0

Typeset in Adobe Garamond by M Rules
Printed and bound in Great Britain by
Clays Ltd, St Ives plc

Papers used by Piatkus are from well-managed forests
and other responsible sources.

MIX
Paper from
responsible sources
FSC® C104740

Piatkus
An imprint of
Little, Brown Book Group
Carmelite House
50 Victoria Embankment
London EC4Y 0DZ

An Hachette UK Company
www.hachette.co.uk

www.piatkus.co.uk

To Anna

Thank you for your support and believing
in this book and this series.
You are truly wonderful.

Chapter 1

A gust of winter air hit my face so hard it felt like God had reached down and slapped me. The cold hurt. Hurt so deep that hugging my black jacket around me did nothing to ward off the intense chill.

The creak of my father's casket being lowered into his grave pierced my ears as I watched it gently sway and wobble, the flowers atop shaking as it descended further and further into the ground.

Everyone was leaving. Turning and walking back to their cars. They'd likely go back to my step-mother's house for mini sandwiches and talk about my father as a friend or colleague.

Not me. I simply stood. Alone. No one looked at me. No one even attempted to make eye contact. They all just walked away.

The burning in my stomach was the only thing that reminded me this wasn't a dream. Wasn't a nightmare even. It was real. Last week, my father, my house, and my soul were ripped from me. Whoever said the truth will set you free clearly had never experienced such truth. Like the truth that I'd fallen in love with two men, only to be betrayed by both. Or the truth that my step-brother was violent and walking free.

I absently ran my fingertips along my cheek where he'd hit me. It was mostly healed. But the memory stuck. I didn't know if I was number from the Colorado cold or from shock. Shock I hadn't quite kicked yet. Despite having a little time to get used to these new truths and facts, it still hadn't sunk in. I'd stopped counting the hours, because it was too much to think through. All I knew was that it was days ago my father died. Days ago, I'd watched my house burn to the ground. Days ago, the last part of my heart had been torn from my body and I'd lost the second man I'd ever loved.

Alone.

I was all I had left. And I really wanted to demand a recount.

"Lana Case?" a balding man with thick-framed glasses asked.

"Yes?" My voice was little better than a croak.

"I'm Greg Simpson, the attorney for the Case-VanBuren estate."

I nodded. Of course, my father and step-mother would have an attorney. His name had come up a few times over the years. Greg had been a part of the "Case-VanBuren union" since my father married my step-mother, Anita. It was no surprise he was here. Especially since the reading of his will was set to happen in the next hour.

"I'm sorry for your loss," he said. I wanted to be polite. To say thank you, but my mouth refused to move. Just like the rest of me.

Anita and Brock played the part of grieving family well as they headed my way. The short manicured grass squished under my heels and I couldn't decide which instinct to trust, flight or fight. Unfortunately, neither came. And I stood. Still.

"We better be on our way," Anita said to Greg, not sparing me a glance. Not that I wanted one from her. "I didn't think you'd show up, Lana," she snapped my name like spitting poison from her lips. "What with those charges you pressed, I would assume you were far too afraid to be near my son."

Her tone was light, yet challenging. Any moment, she'd adjust her oversized black hat and start studying her nails like the fact that her son had assaulted me was no big deal. Brock had muscled his way into my home, hit me, and would have done far worse if I hadn't gotten away. He had posted bail and was out of jail for now, but I wouldn't cower away.

For once, the numbness worked to my advantage. No matter how afraid I was, I'd never let it show, especially to Brock and Anita.

"I look forward to discussing this matter more in front of a judge."

Brock scoffed and crossed his arms. "You think this assault charge will stick against me? You invited me into your home, and from what I recall, you tripped and fell."

He was such a snake. He was the epitome of plain. From his dull brown hair to his dead eyes, he was impotence dressed up in an expensive suit. The way he wove lies so easily was more terrifying than his appearance. Because Brock was nothing if not convincing. But he wouldn't get away with it this time. I'd filed the paperwork, given my statement, and now I had to wait. With the holidays and general slow speed of court cases, it wouldn't be until after the New Year that we'd stand before a judge. It would be his word against mine, but I had a couple firemen on my side who had witnessed the aftermath. They may not have seen Brock hit me, but they saw me run from the house screaming for help. Holding on to that fact gave me more strength.

"I guess we'll see who the judge believes then."

"Or, we could settle out of court," Anita said. Brock went to argue, but she shot him a look before refocusing on me. "Why don't we come to an arrangement just between us? No need to drag this mess out longer than it needs to be."

I tried not to show my surprise. Anita wanted to settle out of court? The only reason she'd do that is if she knew I'd win. Brock would finally get punished for hurting me, and they both knew it.

"How much will it take, Lana?" Greg asked. "I'm sure we can come to a reasonable sum."

My chapped lips parted and stung instantly from the cold. They were trying to buy me off. While I was running low on funds, and currently had no house, I had enough for the cheap motel I was in, and hopefully enough to make it a couple more weeks until the insurance money from the fire came in. This was bigger than money. It was holding Brock responsible for what he'd done.

"No amount of money will change my mind. You hurt me." I looked Brock dead in the eye and tried not to tremble from his vicious stare back. "It's time you take responsibility for that."

A low snarl broke from him, but Anita cut him off quickly.

"Surely, you must want something," she asked, annoyance coating her words.

There was only one thing I did care to discuss. "My father carried a picture in his wallet," I said, forcing my voice to carry enough steadiness. Anita and Brock this close to me made sickness rise in my gut. My cheek still hurt from where the bastard hit me, and he wasn't even trying to hide a smile at his handiwork. It was all I could to not flinch at the memory of his fist crashing over my cheekbone. Or any of the other awful memories he'd left me with.

No. Stay strong. Stay present.

"You're not getting near your father's wallet," Anita scoffed.

"I don't care about anything else. I just want to know if he has that picture still. It's of me and my mother and him."

Anita raised a brow. "Why would he have that?"

"He always carried it," I said again. "And after my house burned down, it's all I have left of my family." Venom laced my veins, since I wasn't sold on the fact that they didn't have something to do with it. Brock may have been spending the night in jail when the flames went up, but the VanBurens weren't innocent. Not in much of anything.

Anita leaned in and rasped, "You lost your family a long time ago."

I tried not to let that sting, but it did. Because she was partly right. I'd lost my sense of family, my father, years ago. Only now, he was physically gone from the world.

With an exasperated sigh, she said, "Fine, if I find the picture, you'll drop the charges?"

"No," I said quickly. "This isn't a bargain. I just want the photo."

It was of no use to her, and even though I knew it was a long shot, I had to try for it.

Anita's eyes met Greg's and she said, "Let's go." Before she turned, she finished with, "I guess this is goodbye, Lana. No reason we need to see each other again."

"Until court," I said.

She scowled. "Unless you change your mind about the charges against Brock."

"I won't."

While I would love nothing more than to never see either one of them again, I would happily show up to plead my case against

Brock when the time came. I could wait. I'd been waiting a long time, a few more weeks or even months was nothing.

Anita and Greg began walking away, but Brock took one step toward me. His cold breath hit my face and I stifled the need to vomit.

"I haven't heard from Erica," he said.

"Then maybe you should take a hint. She left you."

"Yes, and don't think I've forgotten who's to blame for that." His eyes narrowed on me, and as much as I hated it, that familiar fear rose up in my chest. It took all my effort to beat it back down. "If you think she'll testify against me, you're wrong."

For a split second, a look of worry flashed over his face. He was scared. Because he knew, just like I did, that if I called Erica, she would testify on my behalf for the breaking and entering. She may not have known the kind of man Brock was at the time, but she'd realized quickly after he'd broken into my home and fled. Fled in a car she was driving. Which made her an accomplice. The single reason I wasn't going after Brock for that as well. I would never want to put Erica in that position. If the DA went after Brock for the breaking and entering, they'd likely tie Erica into it as well. She was a single mother who got caught up with the wrong man and didn't know what he was doing. I wouldn't let her go down for that. So, the assault charges against Brock would have to be enough.

"Blame me all you want, this time, there's no getting around the truth," I said. My gumption was wearing thin, and I just wanted to be away from him. Masking my fear took a lot of energy. But I tried. I would try forever.

"Brock," Anita called. "Let's go. We don't want to delay the reading of the will." I frowned and Brock just smiled and headed towards his mother. "Oh, don't worry, Lana," she said loudly. "You're not in the will. So don't bother coming."

I looked at Greg and he shook his head in agreement. "It's true. Just Anita and Brock are named."

I swallowed down the ache in my throat. I didn't care about material items. Money. Any of it. But my father was dead, and it was the final confirmation that I meant nothing. They didn't speak another word as they continued on their way.

I stood, staring, as the last creaking inch of the levy placed my father six feet under. My phone buzzed in my pocket and I looked at it. The police station again. They'd called a couple times asking the same questions. Questions about my father and his life and why he would want to commit suicide. I shoved the phone back into my pocket, deciding to call them back later. All I could tell them was the same thing I'd already said from the start:

I don't know.

Carter Case was many things, but opting out of life early wasn't his style. Something the police seemed to be in line with, as this investigation into his "suicide" was proving to be extensive.

But what did I know? I didn't know my father. Hadn't for a long time. Maybe Anita was right. I never had a family.

Yet, as I stood there, staring down at my father laying to rest, I couldn't turn to walk away. Instead, I stepped closer. A morbidity laced my thoughts as I stared at the ground, looking down at the casket that concealed the one man I once thought would save me from the world. My stomach punched with pain. He had never saved me from the world ... and it turned out, I couldn't save him back.

But I couldn't leave him. Not yet.

A gust of wind kicked up and rustled the flowers on top of his casket. Little flecks of dirt sputtered over the clean roses, and seeing those brown spots hit the white petals angered me. Made tears start all the way from my toes and slowly work up my body, gaining weight until they hit my eyes.

I sat in one of the many empty white chairs, continuing to stare down at him.

In the ground. Gone forever.

Pressing my knees together to ward off the chill, I frowned when a drop of water hit the flowers. Then another. It seemed so vicious. Putting something so alive, so beautiful in the ground only for it to get covered by dirt.

More water fell from the sky, and I watched it dampen the roses until they wilted from the weight of the rain. The slapping of raindrops hitting the top of the coffin echoed a sharp melody. The sound was hypnotizing.

He was gone . . . truly gone.

I watched as the man who had raised me, resting safe inside a wooden box, got rained on. It was the most horrible thing to witness.

His entire life was confined to that one moment, and I couldn't save him. Couldn't ask him anything. Couldn't tell him that no matter what, I loved him. I just watched the rain beat harder down on something I'd never be able to change.

My breath fogged as I exhaled deeply, my hands bunching on my lap. Water poured around me—

Around me. Not *on* me.

I frowned at the ground that was sopping, except for the patch beneath my heels.

I wasn't getting wet.

Glancing up, a large black umbrella was perched over my

8

head, and an even blacker pair of eyes glowed from behind it.

"Jack," I whispered.

He was standing tall, in a dark suit and chiseled frame, holding out the umbrella to shield me from the rain, while he stood beneath nothing but the gray sky, taking a beating.

"Why are you here?" I asked, hypnotized for a whole other reason. His jet hair was sopping wet, drops of water trailing from his head to his striking face, weaving down the five o'clock shadow that masked his high cheekbones. He blinked once, sending another drop dancing along thick eyelashes. All I could was follow the path of rain from his brow to his lips. Soaking. He was standing beneath the storm, while holding out a cover for me to hide under.

My wall.

Shielding me from the harshness that nature – life – was throwing out.

"I'm here for you," he rasped.

Those four words struck my chest like a spear. Four words that made me feel instantly not alone. Four words I would have given my soul to hear a few months ago when he'd walked out on me.

Jack Powell was one of the two reasons my heart refused to beat correctly. He was my first love. My first passion. My first safety net. And he'd taken all three the day he left me.

Once, he'd been the man who helped me find strength. Helped me tackle the demons from my past and push me to be stronger. It broke every emotion I had when he'd left, and rebuilding had been the hardest thing I'd ever done. And I'd done it with his best friend, Cal. Only, Cal was no better than Jack. He may not have left me, but he had deceived me. And my world was in a shambles, because the truth was a nasty thing to swallow.

But the truth was, Jack and Cal had set me up. Had split my life in half and taken turns pursuing me. Problem was, I'd fallen for both of them, and figured out too late that they had agreed to share time in order to have me.

I looked at Jack. Intensity radiated off of him thicker than the clouds and buzzing with even more energy. Being near him tore at my heart so badly that I could hear the seam rip from deep in my chest.

"I don't need you," I whispered, rising to stand. He moved to keep me shielded as I turned to face him. "I don't need this either." I grabbed the handle, collapsed the umbrella, and gave it back. Rain instantly battered the top of my head and ran quickly down my face like the spray from a shower.

"I don't want you getting cold and sick," he said.

"*Now* you're worried about me?" I scoffed.

He hit me with a dark glare and stepped forward. "I've always been worried about you."

I wanted to yell and scream and tell him he was full of it. Because he'd watched me cry, heard me beg – beg – for him to stay, and still turned away. The memory sickened me, but it didn't change the outcome.

I'd *begged* for him.

Something a weak person would do. I hated being weak. Tried so hard to feel anything but that single emotion. Which was why Jack was the best kind of sinful pleasure. Because in one breath he made me feel strong – and in another he made me beg. Only he could cause a war between two such powerful emotions. But I couldn't give in now. My father was gone, my world wrecking like a slow moving train collision, and I was on the brink of snapping under the pressure.

"I'm done with you," I whispered.

Wild heat flamed like melting obsidian behind those electrifying eyes. He pushed the chair that separated us out of the way, toppling it over onto the soaked grass, and the force made mud splatter on my ankle. Jack stepped into the newly open path and didn't stop until the tip of my nose brushed against his wet chest.

He pinched my chin and lifted my face to the rain. I stared up at him, eyes fluttering from the drops of water hitting me. His gaze was ensnaring and his expression burned me up as he looked down at me, haloed by the gray sky and thick blanket of rain.

He was an angel. A stark, beautiful angel of darkness.

"Say what you need to say," he rasped. "Be done with me if that's what you want." His hips shifted, pressing into my body and I bit back a moan. "But *I'm* nowhere near done with *you*."

He'd come back into my life last week, and ever since our brief encounter, his presence hadn't left. Rather, it followed me around like aftershocks of lightning. And in that moment, seeing Jack's dark eyes and deep frown, I wanted so desperately to close the few inches between our lips, and hide.

I hated myself for wanting such a thing. He was the man that stole my soul. Lied to me. And left my broken heart behind for his best friend to pick up the pieces.

Yes, I wanted to run and hide. But I didn't know in which direction to do either.

"You shouldn't have come here," I said. "This is my . . . " I stopped the word "mess" from slipping out. Because that's what this was. A mess. Brock, my father's death, the unsolved stalker issue. All of it was crashing down harder than the rain and I glanced at the casket in the ground. All the flowers that were lovely mere moments ago, were ruined.

"This is my father's funeral," I finally got out, shock hitting me, and I had no idea what to do with it.

"I know," Jack said. "And you're not alone."

My eyes shot to his. He was there, had been there, offering shelter beneath his cover of darkness. I missed that shelter. The hot, raw, consuming way I melted into his arms and the world faded away. The same fever that came with his consumption swirled around me in a different way than it used to. Because I knew what I was missing.

Loss.

It was a day of total loss.

I'd had Jack once. Had that shelter. But that was over now. He may be standing there, but I still felt alone.

"Goodbye, Jack." I looked at my father one more time, then walked away, further into the storm.

Pulling my car keys out of my purse, I lifted my chin and prepared to make a clean getaway. My car was only a few more feet away. Almost there . . .

"Lana," Jack said, passing me and stopping by the front of my car, hovering near the driver's side.

"Nope," I said back, focusing really hard on unlocking my door. I couldn't do this. Couldn't be near him. Couldn't talk to him. I was teetering on the brink of tears and anger and sadness and I. Just. Couldn't.

"Talk to me," he demanded, but his tone was softer than usual. Though he still issued a command, the way he said it held an undertone of . . . begging. I shook my head because, clearly, I'd misheard. Jack Powell made others beg. But not him. Not ever.

The umbrella was back up and he was covering me once again . . . the wall he was so good at playing in full force. And the memory of how he once guarded me, while pushing me to be strong, stung like a thousand wasps along my skin.

"Talk to me," he said again.

"I have nothing to say to you."

"Oh, I'm sure you have plenty to say to me." He was right. I likely did. But nothing that would change the past. When I said nothing, he moved toward me, dominance radiating off of him. "You can't avoid me forever."

I glanced up at him, fury and anger and bone chilling sadness enveloping the last ounce of patience I had.

"Sure I can."

His eyes narrowed and he unleashed the dark glare he typically saved for when he was preparing to unleash all kinds of hell . . . or all kinds of lust. I was interested in neither at the moment, no matter how much my body was itching with the need to grab hold of him.

"But you won't." Calm confidence dripped from every word.

I redoubled my efforts of unlocking my car. When did jamming a key into a metal notch become so hard? Maybe it was the intense man staring me down that had my palms shaking. A man that spurred all kinds of feelings and memories I didn't want to tackle. Especially when his hand around the handle of the umbrella gripped tighter. Hands I knew intimately.

He leaned in, crowding me. My little Honda looked like a clown car compared to his broad shoulders and towering frame.

"What do you want from me?" I asked with exhaustion.

"I want you to come home with me and talk to me. I want to listen to you. I want you to listen to me back." His free hand skimmed along my neck. The damp feeling of his fingertips made me shiver, and my cold body instantly ignited with heat. "I want to take this pain in your eyes away."

I wanted that too. So much. Jack was the first man that I'd told about Brock attacking me when I was young. Jack gave me

13

the strength to be honest and took the burden of my secret I'd carried for years away. He was the cure to the poison that had been a part of me for so long. Only now, Jack was a special kind of drug, one that held its own side effects.

"You can't," I said.

"Yes, I can," he said harshly. "You just have to let me. So, let me, Lana."

"Let you?" I scoffed. "Since when do you need to be *let* to do anything?"

His eyes smoldered. "Since you."

That stopped every single thought I had.

He gripped my nape, his palms brushing my wet hair down my back, and he pulled me closer.

"Please, baby," he whispered, his mouth close to mine. "*Let me* fix this."

I choked on a sob. His heat, his scent, was pulling me in like a whirlpool. I'd go around and around until I couldn't breathe ...

"There's nothing left between us to fix," I whispered.

He went instantly still, his challenging stare devouring mine.

"There's much between us. And we *will* discuss it at some point," he said, dropping his hand. I shuddered at the loss.

"No, we won't," I said, the key finally clicked in. I twisted and the locks popped up.

"Yes," he said in his trademark firm tone, "we will."

Shoving away a chunk of hair that blew across my face, I stood tall and eyed him. I was done arguing.

"*I* get to decide when – if – I want to talk to you." I hit him with the best glare I could muster. "You lost the right to tell me what to do when you lied to me."

"It was never a right," he rasped. "It was a privilege."

Needles pricked my veins. For a single moment, the rawness

in his admission clawed at my chest. Jack never tossed out random words. Ever. Which is why my stomach squeezed. He spoke about me, about the control I'd once given him, as an honor. And I believed him. But we were over, had been over, because he'd walked away. That truth delivered another agonizing twist to my entire body.

"Regardless," Jack snapped, cutting into the silent exchange, where I believed he was actually asking instead of demanding. He had a way of effectively yanking me back to the chilly afternoon of reality. "You will face me and we will talk, because your safety is at stake at the very least."

Leave it to Jack and his demands to ratchet up my temperature. Once upon a time, I liked his demands. Because they always came with freedom and left me with strength. Now, I had to remind myself and him that, "My safety, or anything else about my life, is not your concern."

"I disagree completely." His tone dropped an octave. Those dark eyes skated over me leaving a searing heat behind. "Everything about you concerns me."

"Why?" I whispered.

"Because I lo . . ." Jack paused, like whatever he was about to say sliced through him and made him rethink. But his dark mask slid back into place quickly. "Because you are mine."

Mine. It was a single word that held so much weight. But there was an even heavier word I had in my arsenal.

"*Was,*" I said and yanked open my car door. "I *was* yours."

With that, I got in and shut the door on a man I'd once thought to be my future, and drove away.

Chapter 2

I jammed the magnetic card into the slot on my hotel room door and jimmied the handle open. The door gave way really easily, like I didn't even need a key. I stepped into my room. It was cold and sparse, but the ten by ten box with a busted TV and ratty brown carpet was what I called home for now.

I just wanted today to be over. I kicked off my heels and—

"Jesus!" I gasped when I saw a large man sitting on my bed.

"Do you have any idea how easy it was for me to get in here?" Cal asked, his crystal blue eyes fastening on me. Scratch that, I had a large *fire*man sitting on my bed, and he was in navy pants and a matching blue button-up uniform shirt, complete with silver badge and way too much swagger.

"Breaking into my hotel room now?" I said and crossed my arms.

"It wasn't difficult," he said. "Especially since your lock is busted. It's not safe, Lana."

It was the same argument he'd been giving me for the better part of a week. And I'd been successful in ignoring him. Until now.

"You're the only one breaking in!" I snapped.

"That you know of. Either the lock is super shitty due to the quality of this place or someone broke it and has already been in here."

"Could that someone be a blond pain in the ass?" I said, looking at him hard to make my point. *Not* looking at him hard because the way his uniform fit tightly around his strong biceps, with just a hint of the tattoos he concealed beneath barely peeking out. And also not staring an extra second to appreciate that muscular chest leading down to a black leather belt. He stood casually and flexed his hips.

My gaze snapped up, and we both knew what I'd just been caught staring at. But Cal in his fire uniform came second only to Cal naked. Another thing I wasn't thinking about . . .

"I miss you, Kitten." He took a step toward me. "And I think you miss me too."

He delivered a smile so dazzling I rocked on my feet from its power. But when he fired off both dimples, I was swooning.

No!

Damn it, I was losing my mind because I was exhausted. Between the funeral, confrontation with the evil step-mother and her little son too, not to mention Jack's hot gaze that left first degree burns on my skin, I was spent. And in no shape to fight against Cal's charm.

"You should go," I said.

"Okay," he agreed easily. "As long as you come with me."

"No," I said, unable to keep the shaking out of my voice. "We're done, Cal." It was the second time I'd said that in less than an hour. And it hurt just as badly as saying it the first time. Because Cal was right there with Jack when it came to deceiving me. When Jack had left, Cal stepped in and made me believe in love. Believe in myself. Made me hope.

The prick.

He made life so easy. Too easy, because I fell in love with him and gave him all the pieces Jack had left broken, and he'd taken them, and put me back together. Only I found out that he'd made an arrangement with Jack to have his time with me. Apparently, they'd both wanted me and had to work around that. So they'd thought they were giving me a chance to be with each of them, so I could then choose. Too bad I fell in love with both of them.

Cal made the brazen in me rise. He let me claw at what I wanted and hold on tight. He let me have my control, giving me power over myself. He let me run, whenever I needed, but he always came after me.

"I'm not going anywhere without you," he said. "I know you're hurting. I know I fucked up. I know today was hard on you. I would have been there . . ."

I looked him over, registering that since he was in his uniform . . . "You're on duty?"

He nodded. "I came here to take you home with me."

"Cal, I can't," I whispered. Because his home was so warm and welcoming. It felt like him, and if I closed my eyes really tight, I could feel the soft sheets of his bed against my skin and the spicy smell of his skin as he climbed in next to me . . .

I needed these memories to go away, not repeat them. Because I was already losing a losing battle.

"I'm not looking to control you," Cal said, regaining my focus on him. "I'm looking to protect you. Show you that I'm sorry." He stepped closer, the bottom of his shoe scuffing against the carpet. He tucked that stray lock of hair behind my ear. "I'm sorry," he whispered. "So damn sorry. For what you've gone through, what I put you through. Please believe that I never meant to hurt you."

My pulse sped up and my forehead hurt from the deep frown marring it. It was all I could do to keep my eyes from watering. Part of me did believe him.

I took the smallest step toward him.

"I just want to protect you. I'll give you space, but let me at least keep you safe." His voice was smooth, and I knew too well he was playing good cop.

Let him?

Again, the second time I'd heard that. Both Jack and now Cal had spoken to me like this whole situation was in my hands. Like I held the power and dictated what they could and couldn't do. If that were true, why did I feel so weak? So alone?

I looked into those deep blue eyes and, for a moment, remembered how only a handful of days ago I was lost in them. Stared at those same eyes and told him how much I loved him. Funny how life changed in moments. Seconds.

"I don't need your kind of support," I shot the last word out like a bullet. One that clearly got a reaction, because anger laced Cal's face. That rarely happened unless he was feeling out of control.

"A summer-fuckin-breeze could open your motel room door, Lana. What makes you think the person who burned your house down, or Brock, who has shown he has a taste for breaking in to your place, won't find you here?"

I swallowed hard. I had no answer for that. And Cal's need to keep me safe, physically at least, was driving his prime instinct. He let me have control in any other way I needed, but this was one area he'd fight me on until I caved.

"It doesn't matter. You don't have to worry about me anymore. I'm not your problem or yours to save. I can deal with the door, and my life, myself."

"I'm trying," Cal said. "Trying to give you what you need. Trying to give you space. But asking me to sit back while you're in clear danger is not going to happen. I'm not going away. You're more important than anything, and I'm tired of this."

My brows shot up and I wanted to yell at him. To cry. To throw my hands up and scream a little too. "*You* are tired of this? Guess what, so am I. Only you and Jack are the ones who started *this* and I'm not playing anymore!" With a deep breath, I cursed my eyes to stop watering immediately. No way was I showing weakness now. I couldn't let a single ounce of sadness or despair creep out, because once it did, I wouldn't be able to call it back. Facts. I needed to cling to the facts.

"You set me up from the beginning," I whispered. Fact. "You lied to me." Fact. "You used me and passed me between the two of you like some—"

"I'm not going to let you finish that statement," he said with fire. The edge of his voice was something not only my mind, but my body registered. And I hated it. Hated that my own self betrayed me. "I never used you."

He went to reach for me, but I backed away. The look that flashed over his face was so pained it almost brought the threatening tears back up. Anger quickly surged and drowned out the need to cry. How dare he look like *I* was hurting *him*!

"Did you expect me to feel differently?" I asked.

Earlier, Jack had been demanding. Pushing me to believe him. While Cal was silently pleading. They pulled at every emotion I had. Memories flooded each time I caught the faint smell of Jack's cologne or the flash of Cal's dimples. They were imprinted in my mind and I couldn't escape them. In any sense. And I'd tried for the past week.

Cal took a step closer, his big build closing in on me.

"I never want you to feel anything but loved. Come home with me," he whispered. "I don't want you staying here any more than you want to be here."

The last bit of tenacity I had left was dwindling rapidly. Because, honestly, I was ready to give in. Cal was right, I didn't want to be in a shitty hotel. I didn't want to sleep on stiff linen and take cold showers. I wanted to be wrapped up in the man I loved. I wanted my home to still exist. I wanted my life back.

My whole body and mind were at odds with . . . everything.

Cal looked at me, long and deep, and just the sight of him stung my ribs. The wounds of his betrayal were so fresh that every single second I was in his presence was like salt sprinkling over the gaping hole he'd left behind in my chest. And Jack only made it worse. Because while I made amends with the fact I'd never get over him, being in his proximity, feeling his heat, yet being too far away to harness the warmth, was torture. He'd left me. I'd rebuilt with Cal. And now I stood in the same town with two men who possessed equal and different parts of my entire being.

"I'm on shift for the next forty-eight hours," Cal said, as if sensing he was losing me. "You can have the place to yourself. Avoid me all you want, just do it from my house."

I glanced around the tiny room, then at the lock. Could someone have broken it? It was hard to admit that part of me was scared. Had been for a while now. I wanted to be able to sleep through the night just once.

If Cal was going to be on shift, maybe I could compose myself, rest, and be gone before he got home from the station.

It was still a step to take down a path that led me to Cal. And I couldn't help wanting to run straight down that path and jump in his arms, no matter how unwise that was.

"I'll let you flash the lights," he said.

My gaze snapped to his and my brows shot up. He couldn't mean . . .

"The truck is here?"

Cal let those incredible dimples free once more and nodded. He pointed just outside and I walked out the door, around the corner and—

"Whoop-whoop!"

The large red fire truck was parked in the back lot and sounded just a flick of the siren. The lights started flashing, and three guys waved from behind the windshield.

"You drove the fire truck here?" I turned to ask Cal.

Sticking his hands in his pockets, he shrugged. "Figured it was the only way to get you to agree to a ride. And if you barricaded yourself in the room, I was prepared to take out the ladder and carry you out."

A small laugh escaped my lips.

"God, I've missed that sound," he said, staring at my mouth. Cal was so good at making me laugh. And I missed it too.

"Lana!" Dave called, sticking his head out of the side of the truck and waving me over. "I've got twenty bucks riding on the line here. You're killing me!"

Dave smiled and I shot a look at Cal.

"Dave bet that you'd tell me to fuck off," Cal grumbled.

That made me smile. "Twenty, huh? And what do you have riding on my decision?"

Cal's expression was serious when he looked me in the eyes and simply said, "Everything."

Chapter 3

"Remember," Dave called from the truck as Cal walked me up to the front door of his house, "Just because Cal fucked up royally, doesn't mean you can ditch the rest of us. We're doing dinner at the station tomorrow night. Family only, so you better show up!"

Dave's kind invitation knocked on my chest like a fist from the inside trying to break free. They thought of me like family? I'd been to the station a few times back when Cal and I were together and knew firsthand how close all the guys were. And Cal had made me feel like a part of his world.

As we reached the front door, Cal took out his keys and unlocked it, while the truck idled loudly on the side of the street, waiting to take him back to the station. He opened the door and handed me the key.

"I'll be back tomorrow morning to check in," he said. "But there's something inside I think will make you very happy."

I frowned, but when he flicked on the entry light, I saw Harper sitting at the table.

"Oh, my God!" I dropped my small bag and she ran to hug me. "I've missed you."

"I've missed you too," she said, hugging me back.

"I'll see you tomorrow morning," Cal said, then walked down the steps and toward the truck.

"Cal," I called after him. He turned and those blue eyes snared me. "Thank you."

He flashed his rugged smile and nodded once. There he was, giving me space, walking away, just like I'd pushed him to do, all while making sure I was okay.

I couldn't think of that for long because with a quick wave to the truck, Harper yanked me inside and we were sitting on the couch, knees bent and catching up.

"Oh, my God," Harper said, taking my hands in hers. "I'm so sorry, the avalanche made it impossible to get here until now."

I gave a little squeeze back. She was warm and smelled like fresh snow and citrus shampoo. God, I missed my best friend. The weather and snow had made traveling back here difficult, but I was so happy she'd finally made it.

"So, I hear Jack and Cal have taken the title as your own personal guard dogs," she said. She must have heard that from the gossip mill that ran around the station.

"They refuse to leave me alone."

"Can't really blame them," she muttered.

"Yes, I can," I said quickly.

"You're right. You totally can."

Harper knew the gist of what had gone down between Cal, Jack, and me. She also obviously knew about the fire, since it was her house too that burned. Luckily, she had a good deal of her personal stuff at her parents' house, where she'd been visiting. When I called to tell her about my father's death, she scrambled trying to get back, but the snow had her caged in until now.

"Did you drive today?"

"Yeah, took most of the day. Stupid snow," she said. "I'm sorry to hear about your dad. I can't believe he died the same day our house burned down. Do the police think it's linked?"

"Right now, they're treating the instances as separate," I answered. My father's death was unofficially deemed a suicide, as of this moment. The fire report on the house was still underway. Though foul play was expected, we were still waiting to hear what the arson investigation turned up.

"So, the police are still investigating your dad's death?" she asked. Her neatly curled hair hung like glossy curtains around her face. For spending the majority of the day in a car, she looked amazing. As usual. Her ivory skin was fresh and smooth, her eyes rested and calm. Whatever she had, I wanted some. Though I hadn't glanced at a mirror in a while, I felt withered, and it showed.

"Yeah. They aren't officially ruling my dad's death a suicide until they do some more tests."

"What kind of tests?"

"I don't know. Gun powder residue and bullet matching stuff." It wasn't that I didn't care. I did. I just didn't know what to expect. If my father really killed himself, what would that mean? And if he didn't? My brain couldn't process all the outcomes or scenarios. I was waiting for facts because I couldn't deal with any more speculation.

Facts.

The single tool I had to keep my sanity in all areas of my severally crumbling worlds.

"I'm sorry I wasn't at the funeral," Harper said. "I'm sorry for a lot of things. I should have been around more, Lana."

"It's not your fault," I said.

"Were Anita and Brock assholes to you?"

Just my reaction to their names and recalling the encounter I'd had with them earlier by my father's grave told me it would take a dose of strong liquor to wash down the bitter taste they'd left behind.

"No more than usual," I said around a strangled breath. "My father carried a picture in his wallet. At least, I think he still did. It was of my mom and me and him. I asked if I could have it and Anita basically told me to fuck off."

"Bitch," Harper said.

I didn't know why I was holding on to a simple picture. I just wanted something of my dad's, some memory that wasn't tainted.

"What about the fire? Any word?"

"Hopefully, in the next day or two we should get the official fire report. They're pretty sure it was arson, but the details will come in soon."

Harper nodded. "Now we just have to wait for the insurance to kick in. They'd said that they'd have a check for us around New Year's, right?"

"Yeah, right around there." They were taking their sweet time with this and the New Year was still a few weeks away. "Will you tell me about you?" I asked. "I've missed you, and I just feel like so much has been going on in your life and I know nothing about it."

Harper gave a guilty look, then a shy smile. "Now isn't the time to talk about it."

"Ah, now is the perfect time! Please, Harp. Give me something."

"Okay ... I eloped."

I wish I was drinking something so I could have spit it out. "What? When? With who?"

"Rhett. We've been seeing each other and I . . . love him. But we had some issues. Okay . . . I had some issues. But he came to see me at my parents. Fought for me. Refused to leave until I admitted the truth."

"And what's that?"

"I love him," she said. "So much. I didn't think it was possible. But I do. He makes me laugh. Makes me think life can be fun and easy. But he challenges me to be better. He's intense and a little wicked, and I just love him."

Listening to my best friend rave about her husband. Wow. Husband. Was incredible. It also made me zone in on certain words.

Intense.

Casual.

Fun.

Challenging.

It was Jack and Cal. Two sides to the coin and Harper got it in one man.

"I'm sorry," Harper whispered. "I didn't mean to sound all happy. I was going to wait to tell you, with everything going on—"

I took her hands in mine. "I'm glad you told me. And I'm so happy for you."

"What about you, Lan?" Harper glanced over her shoulder at the door. The same door Cal had just been standing in before leaving me secure in his home. "What are you going to do?"

"There's nothing to do," I said. "I'm done."

"With Cal or Jack?"

"Both."

"I don't think they'll take that as an answer."

"I don't care," I said. "They hurt me. Betrayed me." A sob

27

broke my throat and I couldn't help it. I tried shaking it away, but it wouldn't budge. The pain was stuck. All I could do was try to talk around it. "I gave them everything. I believed them."

"I know," she whispered, and pulled me in for a hug. Whatever gates that were holding back all my emotions, opened. Harper's arms tightened around me and a few tears fell. Then a few more.

I cried for every hour of every day since I'd gotten stood up on that damn blind date and my life changed forever. Cried because I loved Cal. Because I still loved Jack. Cried because I hated how much I loved them.

"I hate them," I whispered. "I hate them so much because I love them and it . . . it feels like I'm dying. Like I can't breathe."

"I know," Harper cooed and stroked my hair.

"My dad is dead. Everything is gone."

"I know," she whispered again.

"Please," I begged. To who or what, I didn't know. I just knew in this moment, I couldn't fake a smile anymore. "Please make it stop."

The hole was eating away and there was no fight left in me. I was tired. To my core tired of fighting. Tired of trying.

"I wish I could," Harper said and adjusted to make me face her. "This is hard." She cupped my face. "But you, Lana Case, can handle this."

I shook my head. "I can't."

"Yes, you can. You're a survivor."

More tears flooded. I didn't feel like a survivor. I felt like someone who was failing.

"What do I do?"

"You do whatever you have to do to get through this. Because you will get through this." Harper forced me to look at her and repeated. "Do you hear me? *Whatever it takes*. This is your life, *you* decide. *You're* in control." She examined me and finished with, "You also need to get some sleep. You look exhausted."

I felt exhausted. I'd also never felt more lost in my life. I hugged my friend and just repeated her words in my mind:

Do whatever it takes to get through this . . .

"Breakfast for dinner is the best idea ever," Mark said, digging into his plate of food. His mustache had really come in since the last time I'd seen him. The other fire guys sat around the table, passing syrup back and forth for their waffles.

It was so familiar it warmed a very cold part of my chest. Family. This was what family was like. Gathered around the table. Talking. Eating. Being in the middle of the kitchen, everyone crowed around a big circular table, it was hard not to feel welcome.

"It was the best thing to make, since Cal can only handle making scrambled eggs," Dave said, and stuffed a big bite of pancake into his mouth.

"There are no eggs," Mark said.

"Exactly." Dave pointed a fork his direction.

"Shut up," Cal said, and took his seat beside me. Putting an arm around the back of my chair, he placed his other forearm on the table and leaned toward me while talking to Dave. "It's no secret I can't cook."

"Not even breakfast?" Mark asked, then shook his head. "Lana, when you're ready for a real man, you let me know. I can cook any meal." Mark winked, purposefully pissing off Cal, and I laughed.

"I can barbecue you breakfast," Cal said in my ear with all the confidence in the world.

For a moment, I got caught up in the fluid easiness of the moment. The way he looked at me, tossing a few winks out and melting my heart with that sly smile was enough to make me ache at the loss of how things used to be. Even the way he sat next to me was possessive in a simple way. A comfortable way that told the world I was his.

But I'm not. Not anymore.

"You alright?" Cal whispered into my ear, while everyone else held conversations around the table. I looked at him. Those blue eyes laced with concern. I couldn't help but be honest.

"Not really," I whispered back. I could tell he was on the brink of asking why, but I just gave a tight smile and refocused on my food. I didn't want to talk about how the reminder of how this love, this sense of family with Cal, was pulling at my bones until I felt my joints were on the brink of crunching.

Dinner passed in a haze. Everyone talked and laughed.

"So, Rhett and Harper are on their honeymoon for a few weeks, huh?" Mark asked. "Does that mean I have to stop hitting on her?"

Everyone laughed.

Last night, Harper had told me she was going to postpone her and Rhett's honeymoon, but I insisted she go. No reason she needed to sit here and watch me wallow and cry all over the place.

"No, you can. I'd love to see Rhett kick your ass for that," Dave said.

"That guy has got it bad," Mark said.

"Of course he does, he married her," Cal chimed in. Mark's playful smirk zeroed in on Cal.

"Speaking of guys who've got it bad," Mark said. "Did Cal show you the art project he made for you yet, Lana?"

Surprise lit my face and Cal grumbled something like "shut the fuck up" to Mark.

"No, I haven't seen this art project?" I said with wonderment, glancing at Cal.

"Dinner's over," Cal announced, and took my hand, helping me stand.

"Aw, don't be sad, big guy," Mark said. "The glitter was a nice touch. I think she'll like it."

"There was no glitter," Cal defended, then marched me out of the kitchen, down the hall, and into his room. The memories instantly flooded from the last time I was in this small area at the station. It was on this bed that Cal and I had sex for the first time. I'd tasted his entire body and he enveloped me in all that strength. Now, he simply sat down, and coaxed me to sit beside him.

"You have to tell me about this art project now," I said, trying to go for a lighter topic.

"It's not a project," he said, and bent to grab something from beneath his bed. "I ordered this, then just put a few pictures in it."

He handed me a large book. It was red with a matte finish, and when I opened it, tears instantly sprang to my eyes. There, on the first page was a picture of Cal and me. Smiling and happy. I turned, and on the second page was a picture of me on the ladder, wearing Cal's fire gear. That was the night he'd taken me over a hundred feet off the ground, and let me rise above all the problems that had been weighing me down.

I covered my mouth with my hand.

"You made me a scrapbook," I whispered.

"It's not much." He leaned over and looked at the page I was staring at. "I remembered your face when you saw all the pictures Aunt Bea brought out of me, and I wanted you to have a place you could put your memories."

I folded my lips together to keep the tug of pain at bay. Bea was Cal's aunt and the nicest woman I'd ever known. She'd taken me in from the first day I'd met her. Her hugs could cure cancer and she was the kind of mother, friend, aunt, anyone would be lucky to have.

She'd raised Cal since he was a kid after his mother died. She'd also basically raised Jack, since his father was an abusive bastard that lived right across the street. And she'd loved both of them dearly.

"I've never had a scrapbook," I said. I couldn't even get a picture of my father. Let alone have a book of memories. Mostly because there were very few memories that were worth keeping. Until I met Jack and Cal that is. Then life had changed. And I wanted to remember the good times. Because they gave them to me. And now Cal was giving me even more.

"Thank you," I said, as I looked at Cal and clutched the book against my chest.

"You're welcome." He trailed the back of his fingers along my jaw and I closed my eyes and leaned into the touch. When I opened them, he hadn't moved. Hadn't closed the small gap between our mouths.

"Cal," I said his name and those blue eyes lit up with hope. I couldn't deny the addiction I had for this man. I pressed my lips against his and fell apart at the instant warmth of his soft kiss.

Gently touching, stroking those fingers down my neck, he licked the seam of my lips and I opened to take a taste of him. The slightest touch of his tongue was enough to make me moan. I missed him. So badly that my heart was beating in sections. One broken piece thumped, followed by a second broken piece. It hurt so much. The sting of the wound pulsing with . . .

Hope.

I pulled back. "I can't."

I was sad. Confused. And I didn't know where to start with healing, or if it was even possible. Jack was back, the arrangement he and Cal had made was out, and I was sitting there, clutching to the idea of a future, of family, that Cal literally put in my hands. I didn't want to let it go, but it wasn't mine to embrace.

Not anymore.

"Will you take me home?" I asked. As soon as the words left my mouth I realized that I didn't have a home. But Cal answered anyway.

"Yes."

With that, he rose to stand and helped me up. I clung tightly to my book, terrified to my core that it would only ever be filled with the memories of what could have been.

Chapter 4

Cal had gotten the rest of the night off and drove me back to his place in silence. My body was humming, my mind was in chaos, and the hot shower did little to ease any of it.

I rested my head against the shower wall and exhaled. The "wall" was made of dark gray stones and looked more like a walk-in exotic cave than a shower stall. It suited Cal's taste, since this was his master suite. From the furniture to the décor, everything was rugged and masculine.

I was surrounded by the man I'd just pulled away from. I couldn't get that blue gaze out of my mind. Worse, I didn't know what lay behind it.

After washing my hair and body, I now smelled like Cal and the familiar soap I'd come to know so well. I couldn't escape him, even if that was my goal.

I closed my eyes and let the water continue to hit my back, yet nothing eased the tension or guilt.

The sound of bare feet hitting the smooth stones of the shower floor smacked my ears. The one man I was terrified to look at came in behind me.

"Cal," I whispered, keeping my head against my forearm and

forcing tears away. I should tell him to leave. To try to cover myself. Both were pointless. A large part of me didn't want him to leave. I wanted him to stay. I wanted to yell at him. Get all the hurt out.

We are already done I reminded myself, yet nothing felt further from the truth.

The real world was a bitch and came with a past, and that was something we'd have to get back to. Forgiveness was one thing. Moving away from the pain another. And I was willing to do both. Was trying to do both. But it didn't change the future. And the fact that it was waiting for me right outside this house, and I couldn't take Cal with me to it.

Yet, in that moment, all I felt was stuck and horrible and I just wanted to run.

I felt Cal's big body against my back. His tee shirt and jeans scratched against my bare bottom. He'd walked in clothed? He wasn't looking for sex then, just to hold me?

The thought sucked me further into the need to feel him. Get lost in him. But I couldn't even look at him.

"I'll always chase you," he whispered in my ear, then kissed the back of my neck. He either read my mind or acknowledged what had just happened, because that's what I'd done. I'd run away and Cal had come after me.

"I'm lost," I admitted.

"Never, Kitten." He gently cupped my shoulders in his hands and turned me to face him. "I'll find you."

A tear pricked my eyes as I looked up at him. His white T-shirt was getting soaked and his jeans were no better, but he stood there, looking down at me with blue eyes full of under-standing and determination.

"There's so much I want to say," I admitted. Even with the

world and all its problems, like my house burning down and my father's death, there was only one thing I needed to wrap my brain around right then. And that was Cal. "I'm sad. So unbearably sad. And I love you. I love Jack too ... I never stopped. And I hate this."

It was a mess. A loss either way I spun it.

"I know."

I shook my head, my wet hair moving along my back with the action. "How are you like this? How can you be so calm?"

"Because Jack and I put you in this situation. I've known from the beginning about your feelings for him. I know you have to sort things out. But I'm not giving up on us."

"This is fleeting," I said. "There's too much badness to move on or to fix anything. This will all end the second we step away from each other."

"I'm set to change your mind on that."

He pulled me into his arms and wrapped me up in the strength I'd gotten lost in so many times. A warmth like his was unmatchable.

"Don't move on, just move towards me," he rasped, his lips hovering over mine. He'd said something similar in the past when he was there, helping me move past Jack. Without thinking, I did just that, taking a step to press my wet body further against Cal's. His handsome face gave a tentative grin as his lips brushed mine. "That's it, Kitten. Come to me."

He coaxed in such a way I couldn't deny. His mouth snagged mine and took a deep taste. He was everything warm and safe, and I wanted him so much. My chest didn't settle right without Cal. He was an anchor and promise I'd come to rely on. He made me feel not so ... alone.

"I can't do this," I said, and pulled away, but he wouldn't let

36

me. His arms tightened and kept me close. "I can't promise you anything. I can't commit to you," I said. It hurt too much still.

"It doesn't matter," he said against my lips. "I'll take you however you'll allow me."

"How can you say that?"

He looked at me like the answer was simple. "Because I love you, Lana."

God, I loved him too. So much. And Jack was forever in the background of my feelings. I wouldn't ever commit to either of them, but that wasn't the point. What we had was beyond titles and norms. I'd been changed since the day I met Jack, and again when I'd fallen for Cal. One thing that didn't change was the fact that I couldn't get over either of them, and it was tearing me down the middle.

But I'd get through this. I had to. Denying Cal went against my instincts as acutely as denying my lungs air. I couldn't. Didn't want to. Because everything in my body and soul reached out for him.

He slowly ran his lips over mine. When I parted for him, he surged his tongue deep, pushing against my teeth for greater access. I gave in. He kissed me so hard, yet so slowly. And I met every stroke of his perfect mouth.

I kissed him with everything I felt. With an apology I couldn't say and all the logic that didn't matter. I kissed with passion and desperation. Confusion and lust. I needed him. Needed him to need me back.

"I want to feel you," I whispered.

He peeled off his soaked shirt, then his jeans, and tossed the material in the corner with a slosh. I ran my hands along his hard wet torso, up to his chest. When my palms brushed over the ridges of his abs, he sucked in a breath, and all the strength he had flexed further.

He was slick and hard and perfect. I could touch him forever. Leaning in, I skimmed my lips over his bicep and the tattoos I knew intimately. His big hands splayed over my ass, pulling me closer. We were lost in each other's slow moving touch.

I kissed his muscles the way I could his mouth. Licking and sucking. Tasting those tattoos and moving toward his chest.

He moaned my name and his grip on me tightened.

Loving on him made my knees tremble and my stomach flutter. The water felt a degree cooler because my skin was heating by the second. Everything about Cal turn me on. I was wet and aching, and just the taste of his strong frame had me ready to beg to be surrounded by him.

I kissed his pecs, paying special attention to his nipples and the hard ridges of his upper abs. His fingers slid up my back and tunneled into my wet hair. His chest rose on a heavy inhale, like he was happy to have my mouth on him. Almost as happy as I was to have it on him.

"I need to be inside of you," he rasped.

"Yes," I said against his slick chest.

He spun me so quickly, I barely knew what'd happened. But when he pressed his hard cock against my ass, I moaned and went to reach back to feel him. He caught my wrists and put them on the wall in front of me, bending me over slightly.

"I mean what I say, Lana." One brawny arm wrapped around my stomach while the other covered my breasts. "But remember that I'm fighting for what's mine. And I'm not going to be gentle about it."

The tip of his cock nudged my entrance, and I looked over my shoulder and saw his blue eyes blazing with heat, and it was all the warning I had before he surged inside of me. I gasped as he filled every inch of my core and hit so deep. I would have rocked forward if not for my hands bracing myself on the wall.

"*You* are mine," he said in my ear, pulling all the way out and thrusting to the hilt once more.

I gasped at the rough and slow sensation of feeling Cal all around me. In me. He had a softness and kindness in him that melted my heart, but an intensity and heat that made me shudder. He was all alpha male, claiming what he thought to be his.

Me.

He surged deeper, but kept his erotically slow pace, turning my blood to fire, and I could feel every tiny nerve spark to life. Sheathed tight within me, he titled his hips up, hitting the end of my sex and my sanity. He was everywhere, a part of me, and I was drowning in him.

Every drop of water felt like a gallon. My skin was sensitized and vibrating. I felt every touch, heard every breath.

The hand on my stomach dipped between my legs. His teeth grazed my neck when he said, "Does this still feel fleeting?" He parted my folds between two fingers and ran them up and down. "This right here? My cock in you ... " he delivered another upward glide and I moaned. "I feel you, feel how this perfect pussy weeps when I move away ... " he pulled out slightly and I clawed at the wall in desperation. Wanted to scream for him to stay deep. I felt his smile against my neck. "I know what you need. What you like ... I feel it. Every fucking moment of every day. I feel this ... " he surged deep, right where I wanted him. "I live to be right here." He stirred his hips and my head lolled back. He was playing my body like he owned it. Because he did. He knew it, and so did I. "Am I wrong?"

"No," I said around fast breaths. "No, you're not wrong. You know me."

A satisfied rumble broke from his chest. He took one of my hands from the wall and placed it between my legs. Pulling half way out of me, he coaxed me to grip the base of his cock while the crown stayed inside my core.

"I want you to feel me sink into you," he said, slowly pushing forward.

"Yes," I whispered. My fist slackened so he could go deeper, but with every agonizing inch he took, I felt the connection, keeping my fingers on his shaft as he disappeared back into me.

"Now, tell me who makes you feel this." He shot up with a strong thrust and snapped my body to full alert.

"You do," I sobbed. The ecstasy was so blinding I could barely speak. Could only shudder and tremble from the fast release that was creeping up my spine at a painfully slow pace. It was too much and not enough.

"Cal . . . " I whispered his name. "Cal."

It was the only word that made sense right then. The only thing that held my focus. He was so ingrained on every cell I had that I couldn't imagine my body without his.

"Best damn thing I've ever heard," he rasped against my neck.

"More," I begged. "Please. I need it. Need you."

He adjusted me so that both my hands were back on the wall. Reaching around to grasp my breast in one hand, the other was back between my legs, covering my clit.

"Hold on and I'll give it to you." With that, he pounded hard. Over and over, sinking that big cock into me while rubbing the sensitive bundle of nerves in tight, fast circles.

"Oh, God. Yes. Please don't stop."

"Never," Cal rasped and clutched me tighter. Our wet bodies sliding against each other and the sound of our skin meeting was an intoxicating symphony. I was in his strong grip, like a doll

40

writing in his strength. And I gave in to that strength. Let him hold me. Turned my pleasure, my body, and my soul over to him and his power. "I'll never stop."

I believed him. The desperation and fierceness in his words snapped my will to hold out. My body sang like a plucked chord of a harp and trembled with pleasure as my release overtook me.

"Come on, give it all to me." Tilting and stirring, he hit every pleasure point I had.

My orgasm spurred his because he plunged harder. As if wanting to feel exactly how he made me feel. And that was cherished.

"Keep coming. Don't stop," he demanded.

There was a raw edge to his plea, like he knew, just like I did, that when this moment was over, life was waiting for us. He wanted to stay in it as long as possible. And I felt the same way.

Over and over, my pleasure just hummed and continued.

"Love you," he rasped against my wet hair and with a deep thrust, I felt his hot jet of release take over. I felt claimed. Protected. Wanted.

Breathing hard and kissing my neck, my hair, he slowly withdrew and turned me to kiss my face. My legs were like jelly, but Cal just held me.

I stood, wrapped in his strength, and reveled in the softness of it.

Chapter 5

"Good Lord, honey," a sweet voice rang out.

I struggled to open my eyes. Once they finally cracked, I was hit with the bright light of day and Bea's round face beaming down at me. Her short gray hair swung around her plump cheeks and her florescent pink coat and matching knit hat were enough to blind me.

"You look tired," she said and helped me sit up. I didn't know if that was a joke, since she'd woken me up to say that. "Cal called me. He had to go back to the station today. Something about being short staffed and a small house fire on the other side of town."

"Oh, okay. Thank you for waking me up." I looked around to grab my things. After last night, Cal had dried me off and put me in one of his T-shirts, and it was so comforting I'd passed out and was dead to the world until now. "I was going to head out anyway."

My brain was scrambled, trying to think of what to do next. I'd slept with Cal last night. I could convince myself it was a goodbye type of moment, but nothing in the way he held me was

42

goodbye. But I'd meant what I'd said about commitment. I couldn't give him one. All the pain and lust had built to a boiling point last night, and after his gift and the calm caring touch he'd delivered, I'd caved.

"Great! Because I was going to see if you wanted to grab a bite." Her cheerful tone made me smile. "Maybe pancakes?"

"Pancakes," I repeated. Funny, we'd just had pancakes last night at the station, but they sounded really good. Just the idea of a warm breakfast made my stomach growl.

"Pancakes sound wonderful, but I had some stuff to do today," I said. I needed to focus on what I could control. Which was almost nothing.

"Like what?"

"I need to find a job." That had been an inevitability. I'd like to find a source of income before all my money was gone, and while I was hopeful the insurance money would come in soon, I didn't want to count on that.

She gave me a half hug. "You will really need a good meal then."

Her blue eyes were kind, and they reminded me of Cal's. So much it was difficult to look at them.

"Come on, honey. I'll just keep pestering you until I get my way," she hugged tighter. "Besides, just because the boys are idiots doesn't mean you're not still mine."

The word hit my heart with so much force I wanted to fall back on the bed. Jack and Cal both had claimed me once, and now Bea was claiming me too?

"Yours?"

"Of course. You're family."

I wanted to argue. To tell her I wasn't and that I didn't have a family, but she just shooed me toward the bathroom and started the shower. Clearly, she wasn't taking no for an answer. Maybe a day out with Bea wouldn't be so bad.

After a few seconds of hot water, followed by a few minutes of ice cold water, I was ready to go. I'd needed the dose of freezing to settle my nerves because just being in that shower had spiked my blood pressure.

I walked out of Cal's house with Bea and got into her car. She sped down the street, heading into town. She was taking the back roads. I'd think she was maybe even extending our drive, if I didn't know better.

"You look horrible, honey."

I smiled. Bea was never one to spare the truth. "I feel horrible."

"I can imagine." She glanced at me, the smell of her was comforting and her sad expression made me straighten my shoulders. I wouldn't be weak. It was time I at least pretended I was alright.

"Do you want to talk about your dad?" she asked softly.

"There's not much to talk about." His death was still a bit surreal. While I had plenty to wait on, like the outcome of the fire investigation, as well as the investigation of my father's death, and a court date for the charges I'd pressed against Brock, I felt a hint of relief.

It may make me an awful person, but Anita had looked me in the eye and wanted to be done. Didn't want to have contact ever again. Which made me happy. I wasn't happy my father was dead, of course, but that invisible rope that kept me tied to the VanBurens had been cut. Not sure if that was looking at the bright side or the horribly morbid side, but my emotions were too scrambled to figure it out. So, I'd take what little comfort I could get while everything remained unanswered and in chaos. The fire, my father's death, questions were swirling and I sat waiting. Waiting for answers. Waiting for two men to give me back my soul.

I wasn't certain the latter would ever happen.

All of the waiting was one thing, but processing what remained of myself after Jack and Cal had put me through the wringer these past several months was the breaking point. Because in every other case, I'd done what I was supposed to.

I was staying strong against Brock. Steeling myself against the fact that someone – likely someone with the last name VanBuren – was actively making my life miserable and endangering me by breaking in and then burning down my home. All that I could deal with, because there were steps to take. And I was taking them. But Jack? Cal? I didn't know where to start. Had no idea what direction to step in, other than backwards.

"Lana?" Bea asked.

I realized water was forming around my eyes again. I shook my head and wiped a hand over my puffy cheeks.

"Talk to me, honey," she whispered. It was the same kind of whisper Cal had when he was pleading with me last night to go with him. The tone in her voice struck something deep that made me angry. Not at her, but at Cal. At Jack. At this whole mess.

"I'm mad," I said honestly. "And I'm trying to be strong, but it hurts. Hurts worse than I ever thought I could hurt. I keep thinking this pain will somehow kill me in my sleep. Like, I'll stop breathing and suffocate from it, but I don't. I keep waking up to the truth … "

"What truth is that?" Bea urged.

"They lied to me," I said. "Both of them. They set me up … took everything I am." I gave a not so humorous laugh. "And I let them. I gave it up willingly. So, what does that make me?"

"It makes you human, honey," Bea said. Small scattered

snowflakes hit the windshield, as we wove down Sycamore Street and continued our slow pace on the back roads toward town. "And I agree with you," she said.

Surprise hit my skin like a blast of hot air. "You do?"

"Hell yeah, I do," she said with some sauce in her voice. "Those boys messed up big time. You have every right to feel the way you do. I think it's good for them to be paying the price it cost of hurting you."

Great, now I wanted to cry for a whole other reason. Bea wasn't even my family and she was supporting me. Letting me feel how I needed to. Telling me it was okay.

"You have to know something, though," she went on. "Those boys have always had each other. It's been them against the world from the start. Nothing has ever come between them."

"I didn't mean to come between them."

"That's not what I'm saying." Bea pulled to the side of the road, parked, and faced me. She grabbed my hand, and there was a desperation in her eyes. "Lana, *you* are their world."

They way her blue eyes searched mine, like I had an answer, made bile rise in my throat. Because I didn't. I had no answer and even less of a clue of how to tackle my life. But she was looking at me like I held some kind of power.

"I don't know what to do," I admitted. Loving and losing Jack had been hell. Now there was baggage between us, the truth between us. And it surrounded me like thick smoke. He'd left to give Cal time with me. And I'd fallen in love with Cal, while never letting go of Jack completely. In the end, they both deceived me. "Love should be about trust and isn't supposed to hurt," I whispered.

Bea frowned and blinked several times. "Oh, honey, I'm with you on the trust part, but you're kidding yourself if you think love doesn't hurt. Love is the worst kind of pain, and I'm sorry to see you go through it, but it means something real is there."

"Was," I corrected.

"Oh?" she challenged in her sweet voice. "You don't love Cal? Jack?"

That was something I wouldn't acknowledge out loud.

"You're in love with two men," Bea answered for me. "That's going to hurt." She gave my hand a squeeze and finished with, "But that doesn't mean you give up on it. You fight for it. Through the pain. Through the hard times. Because if it's real, it's worth holding on to."

For the briefest moment, her words sank in, and I wanted so badly to believe them. To take her advice and run to Cal and get wrapped in those big arms that warmed me instantly. To look at Jack and shiver with anticipation right before his touch landed on my skin.

But it wasn't that simple.

"Do you think this was all a game?" I asked.

She sighed and glanced out the window with a shrug. "Honestly? No, I don't. They never would play a game with your feelings. But I'm not surprised how they went about you."

"What do you mean? They took turns like I was a Monopoly board."

"I know it looks that way. But that would make them malicious. Which they aren't."

I tossed my hands in the air, then slapped them on my lap. "I know they aren't. Which is why I'm so mad at them."

She nodded. "In the past, when they both wanted something, they figured out a way for both of them to be happy."

"Like sharing a toy," I whispered.

"You're not a toy, and that wasn't their intent. I think they were both taken by you and didn't know how to react, so they went with logic." When Bea spelled it out like that, I heard pieces of Jack in her tone. How simple everything could be explained, like it had nothing to do with emotion. It's just a matter of logic, is all. Try telling that to my throbbing chest and that big empty place where my heart used to be.

"Somewhere along the way, they fell in love with you," Bea said. "So, it doesn't matter how it started. They aren't vicious men. They care. But my guess is they had no idea how to handle what they fell into with you."

Breath refused to leave my lungs as I looked at Bea while her words settled over my skin like hot wax. *They* didn't know how to handle *me*?

"That's hard to believe," I said. "Between the two of them, they could handle anything."

She nodded. "That's right. Between to the two of them, they can. But look who's standing between them?" Her eyes pierced mine. Not in an accusatory way, but an enlightened one. "I think part of them is just as lost as you are, honey." She rubbed my hand between hers. The momentary warmth was comforting.

She tugged my seatbelt, making sure it was tight, and threw the car into gear.

"Now, on to the most important question of the day," she said in a happy tone. "Short stack or full stack?"

I smiled. "It feels like a full stack kind of day."

"That's my girl!"

She slowly pulled back onto the quiet road. As if my brain couldn't crank out anymore thoughts, Bea had thrown a wrench in. She was on my side, yet arguing the case for the guys. A mess. Everything was a mess.

Bea stopped at the only yield sign in a five mile radius and looked left and right. There wasn't even house out here. Just trees, snow, and a small intersection.

The car jolted forward violently and a loud crash sounded. Bea lunged forward, her whole body hitting the steering wheel. A crack, like a pencil being broken in half, hummed through the car. Bea screamed in pain.

My seatbelt cut my jarring off short, whipping me back in my seat, my knee banging against the glove compartment.

Bright headlights shone in the rearview mirror. We'd been hit from behind.

"Bea, are you okay?" I asked. She dropped her hands from the steering wheel, grabbed her wrist, and winced.

She hissed, and before she could answer, the sound of squealing tires rang out and then—

Crash!

We were hit again.

Bea yelled as we both lunged forward again. Not only were we hit from behind, we were hit repeatedly . . . on purpose.

The car swayed just a moment, finally settling after the recent hit. I reached over and threw the car into park, then rubbed Bea's shoulder. She was still clamping her wrist, only now her knuckles were starting to swell from where her fingers hit the steering wheel from that second hit.

"I-I'm okay . . . " she said around a bite of pain.

So much anger flared and took over every single cell I had. Looking at Bea, crying in pain, made my fight instinct kick into high gear.

"Son of a bitch," I muttered. It was Brock. It had to be. And he just hurt a woman I cared about.

I looked behind us and couldn't see the car that hit us. Their high beams were on, and I could barely look back without being blinded. But I heard screeching tires and reversing wheels.

No way would I let him near her. I threw off my seatbelt and grabbed my cellphone, quickly dialing 911.

Signal lost.

"Shit!" I tried again.

Signal lost.

The wheels were continuing to reverse, getting further from us. He was going to hit us harder this time.

"Come on, Bea," I said, unclicking her seatbelt and tugging her toward me. I opened my passenger side door, hugged her hard, and scooted her across the seat and out my side. She moved as best she could, and finally she was out of the car and safe on the shoulder of the road. I clicked on my video camera and held my cell phone out to catch the asshole. I refused to sit there while he continued to ram us.

The car was far away, and instead of coming our way, it peeled out fast, kicking up slush, barreling in the other direction, the fall of snow coating it to where all I could see was a flash of white. There was no license plate and barely a shadow of a person behind the wheel.

All I had was a glimpse of a white car speeding away in the snow. Not helpful.

I ran back to Bea's side. Helping her into the passenger side, I buckled her in. The poor thing was holding her wrist and trying so hard not to wince in pain. I got in the driver's side and tried to call 911 again.

Signal lost.

I yanked on my seatbelt and thanked God the car was still running and drivable. I pulled onto the road.

"I can't get a signal, but here in just a mile, service should pick up." I had my phone in my lap, ready to dial emergency as soon as reception came through.

"Who are you calling?" she asked.

"911."

"No," she winced. "Don't do that."

"Bea, you're in pain and—"

"And you're taking me to the doctor, right?"

My mouth dropped and I looked spastically between her and the road. "Of course! I'm going to the hospital."

"Good. We'll figure all this out there." She leaned back in her seat, still holding her wrist. "Will you get ahold of Cal, though?"

My phone blipped with service. I was ready to argue with Bea, but she just looked over at me, those blue eyes watery, and asked, "Please?"

I nodded and dialed.

"Cal?" I asked.

"What's wrong?" he said immediately.

"I'm with Bea, we've been rear-ended. I'm taking her to the hospital."

"I'm on my way. Are you okay?"

"Yes," I glanced at Bea. "Her wrist is hurt, but we're both okay."

A string of curses lit up the phone and I heard Jack's voice in the background. I didn't have time to explain more and needed to focus on driving, so I hung up and headed straight toward the hospital.

"I'm so sorry, Bea," I said.

"Oh, honey, how could this be your fault? You have nothing to be sorry for."

That's when my gut sank. Because this *was* my fault. My presence put Bea in danger. Though I couldn't see the driver, it was

51

no coincidence that my house had burned down, and now we were hit, twice. Someone clearly had it out for me. And I was certain that someone was Brock.

A part of me had thought that with my father's death, this stalking would be over. That Brock would leave me alone. I was wrong.

"I'm so sorry," was all I said again. Because, deep down, I knew this was, in fact, my fault.

Chapter 6

I waited outside the doors to the X-ray room, running my palms over my face. My knees were shaking, my brain hurling thoughts around a thousand miles a millisecond. Poor Bea. She was hurting. And this stupid stunt likely had something to do with me.

My knee hurt from where it'd bumped the glove box, but it was nothing compared to what Bea was going through.

When would this end? I was fighting shadows and losing. The realization that I was totally and completely out of control shot a dose of mind-numbing fear straight through my temple.

I was losing.

Losing my mind, losing the fight, losing everything.

I was right back to being that scared little girl, waiting for Brock to hurt me. Wondering when it would happen again. When he'd choose to barge in and wreck my world. Panic climbed. He was out there, laughing and taking joy in my fear. In the power he had over me. While I waited to be heard and plead my case.

"No," I whispered to myself. The hands on my knees turned to fists. "No," I said louder. I wouldn't let him do this again. Every moment I gave in to the fear, was a moment in his favor.

My chest stuttered on a gasp. No matter how hard I fought it, the panic wouldn't die down.

I was afraid.

And I hated myself so much for that.

No . . . my mind whispered. *Don't give up . . .*

The heaviness of the terror was overwhelming. Kicking against the current and reaching for the surface was no match for the undertow that kept beating me back down.

So, kick harder.

I heard the loud booming steps of heavy boots coming my way. I looked up, and there was Cal.

Tall and strong and plagued with worry on his handsome face. I pulled myself together the best I could and rose to greet him. His steps increased, eating up the distance between us in the florescent lit hall of the radiology wing. Those big arms opened, and instinct took over . . .

I ran to him.

Just for a moment, I wanted to take a break from all that treading and just sprint away from the burden clawing at my ankles.

"Aw, Kitten," he whispered, and swept me up in his massive embrace. Warmth instantly took over. The spicy smell that was all him triggered a calmness I couldn't harness on my own. I got lost and buried my face in his chest as he hugged me tighter, like nothing in the world could touch me.

Too soon, he pulled away and cupped my face.

"Are you okay?" he asked with a catch in his voice.

I nodded and a small relieved smile tugged at his lips. Lips that came crashing down on mine. Surprise took over, but my body registered him as a necessity. I kissed him back, hard and heavy, and with all the fear and exhaustion and hurt I felt. His stubble with thicker than normal. It felt like at least five days' worth and it scraped against my chin. I loved it. I remembered how it felt all those times he'd kissed me before.

His tongue parted my lips and I let him in. Needing to taste him. Needing to let him take an ounce of this ache from me. I clung to him and moved my mouth with his. Tangling his lips with mine, I tried to get closer. To take a deep drink of everything he was offering. The sound of his strong lips hitting mine over and over made my breaths deepen. More. Just a little more.

His groan vibrated down my neck and all the way to my toes.

Home.

He felt like home.

I remembered this well.

Remembered . . .

I opened my eyes and stepped away quickly, my hand coming to cover my mouth like it had betrayed me. Cal just looked at me. His blue eyes shining in a way I hadn't seen them shine in a while. Those gems dazzled with a clear sign of satisfaction.

I wanted to tell him that I was confused. I'd surrendered to another moment of weakness. Fell into a pattern I hadn't mastered breaking, but none of that came out. Because dark eyes caught my attention.

Jack.

He was standing right behind Cal and honing in on me with a look of heat and fury and lust? I didn't know. But a look like that melted my insides while my skin pricked with cold.

"What happened?" Jack demanded. His thick black hair was combed perfectly and all his sharp, starkly beautiful features were on full display, thanks to a recent shave. His dark blue suit was creased to perfection with clean lines and fit his broad shoulders perfectly. He smelled like sex and money and power.

I shook my head, forcing reality back to my brain, and taking an extra step back from the two hulking men in hopes of clearing my mind further. It didn't help.

"We were rear-ended. Twice. The person took off." It must have been Brock but I had no proof, so I went on. "Bea is in getting an X-ray on her wrist right now. The doctor thinks it's a fracture, but not a break."

"Is she hurt anywhere else? Are you hurt?" Jack asked quickly.

"No."

He nodded once, as if that was good enough for him. But the look in his eyes and the way he moved so intently toward me said we were far from over with this discussion.

"We are done doing this your way," he said, taking another step toward me, bypassing Cal. "I've waited for you long enough. It's time you see reason."

That clicked my temper to full force. I'd been terrified a moment ago, and Cal was there to catch me and take it away. Jack just stood there, pushing buttons only he had access to, causing a concentrated dose of strength to shoot through me.

"Excuse me?" I snapped. While his wording irritated me, the rush of power I felt was incredible. I missed this feeling. Hadn't had it since Jack left. He was like my own personal battery, and I'd thrive on the juice while I could.

"Yes. You're actively putting yourself, and now Bea, in danger."

I went to defend myself, but couldn't. Because I worried about the same thing. This was no accident. This was an attack. A repeated attack. All I was lacking was hard proof of who.

"I would never put Bea in danger," I said. Never on purpose. But I had no excuse now. She'd been hurt because I was in the car. I was the target. Not her. And it was clear this wouldn't stop until I made it stop. "It was a white car," I stared. I may not have

56

much more than that, but I would report all I knew. "He hit us once, then reversed and hit us again. When I heard the tires pull away for the third time, I couldn't sit there and let him keep hurting Bea."

Cal looked ready to kill someone and Jack stayed still, rage pouring off of him like slow moving fog.

"You said him. Did you see who it was? Or the license plate?" Jack asked.

"No. I didn't recognize the car either. But it had to be Brock."

"I agree," Jack said.

I glanced at Cal to gauge his stance on this and the knit brow told me he was obviously supporting Jack's thread of thinking.

"I would never put Bea in danger," I whispered again. No matter how many times I said it, the horror of how close she came, we both came, to being seriously injured wouldn't fade.

Heat grazed over my face. Surprise blasted though my blood when I looked up and found Jack running the back of his fingers down my cheek.

"I know, baby." It was the first time his sharp words held a softer edge, and for a moment, I leaned into his fingers tracing my skin. It had been so long since I'd felt his touch. My body instantly recognized it and screamed for more. But I stepped back, refusing to get sucked in once again.

Jack scowled. "You run toward Cal, but back away from me?"

He glared at the distance I'd just put between us like a tangible barrier. I remembered when I'd seen him on the street months ago, before we really started dating. I had backed away from him then. He wore that same look. He'd thought I'd been running from him. Ironically, I wasn't then. It'd taken me a long time and him leaving before I understood what I'd been doing.

I didn't ever shy away from him, I was trying to lure him into the dark corner he provided.

But that was then. Was I running now? Or just seeking that same hiding place and begging him to come with me? The answer didn't matter, because keeping a distance was best. No matter the look it put on his face. A look that made my gut slice with pain.

"I'm not running in any direction," I said.

Jack looked from my eyes to my knees, then back up again. Like he was trying to determine my response based on my stillness. Finally, he said, "Your father was going to sell his company. He had a meeting set up with a buyer after the New Year." He was back to business as usual.

"How do you know this?" I asked.

A sly grin stretched his amazing lips. "Major business deals are no secret."

"Are we supposed to think this information is useful?" Cal asked.

"Yes," Jack replied. "Because the meeting still stands."

I shrugged. "Okay, that has nothing to do with me. He didn't leave me anything."

"Then why have two attempts been made on your life?" Jack countered.

That question was so simple, yet laced with layers of confusion. "I wouldn't say attempts."

That sounded dramatic, and I needed to hold on to any sanity I had left. Words like murder, death threats, and attempts chipped away at the shaky foundation of calm I was sporting.

"The fire was started in your room," Cal said. "We got the report. The arson investigator is going to call you today, but the accelerant was doused all over your bed." He lifted his chin at the big radiology sign behind me. "Not to mention, the person who hit you in the car today was obviously trying to hurt you."

My skull instantly felt ten times heavier. That information, tied with Jack's reasoning was making my skin prick with fear. Whoever burned my house down had thought I'd been home sleeping. Doused my bed with lighter fluid? And if I had been home? I didn't want to think of that. But reality refused to be ignored, and the notion that the car accident Bea and I were in looked more and more like an attempt to injure us on purpose came into focus. Bea was in X-ray right now, in pain. Because of me.

I closed my eyes for a moment and tried to piece out every emotion rolling through me. I was afraid. Trying so hard not to be ... but I was. And it sickened me. I was tired of facing this alone.

The men before me were a special kind of danger all their own and the exact worst thing for me. Yet I craved them. The warmth of Cal and the heat of Jack. But it was time I used my own logic before emotion. I thought of Bea's words. Thought of what Harper told me.

Do whatever it takes to get through this.

"I don't want to put anyone else in danger."

"Good," Jack said. "Then you'll stay at my house."

Cal laughed. The deep chuckle would have been comforting if a stiff glare aimed at Jack didn't accompany it. "Your house, huh? No. She's more comfortable at my house." Cal looked at me.

"Comfortable?" Jack's voice was cool and challenging. "That's a large assumption."

"Not assumption. I know for a fact she likes my bed."

Jack's lips pulled back from his teeth on a pissed off exhale.

"My security system is better than yours," he stated sharply. "Lana's safety is first and foremost. And I have no doubt I can make her perfectly *comfortable* in my home."

"Enough!" I broke in. "This bickering is ridiculous. I didn't even say I'd stay with either of you."

"It's the only logical solution," Jack said.

Cal took a deep breath and clenched his jaw. "Jack does have a good alarm system. You'll be safe there."

I could have sworn I heard Cal's teeth snap around that statement. Jack was satisfied and nodded once. And my options were limited to . . . zero. The risk had heightened after this car accident and the thought of going back to the hotel, or anywhere, alone made dread stream through my muscles.

They both stared at me. Waiting.

With a shallow inhale, I said, "Okay."

"Good." Jack turned to Cal, about to say something, but he was cut off by the doctor approaching.

"I'm looking for Beatrice's nephew?" the doctor asked, looking between Cal and Jack.

"That's me," Cal said and stepped toward the doctor.

When the doctor nodded and started walking away with Cal by his side, Jack said, "I'd like to know what's going on with Bea."

"Are you family?" the doctor asked quickly.

A muscle ticked in Jack's jaw. He shook his head once and the doctor just gave an uncomfortable smile. After an explanation about HIPA and privacy, he went back to talking with Cal, leaving Jack and me behind to watch their backs.

I looked at Jack. Power and strength in a suit ready to bend the world to his will. And he could. But there, in a poorly lit hospital hallway, he stared in the direction of Cal and the doctor with a look of pain on his face.

Jack Powell was all things powerful ... and the only family he had in the world were Cal and Bea. A family that biologically wasn't his, so he stood there, waiting.

It was a terrible feeling. One I recognized well. In that moment, I decided to put all the anger aside and deal with it later. Deal with all my feelings for Jack later. Because, right then, he was hurting in his own way. He needed control. Needed to protect just like Cal did, he just went about it in his own way. And he loved Bea. Very much.

I slipped my hand into his.

He looked at me, then at our hands, but said nothing.

I didn't say anything either. Just stood there, trying this time, to be his wall ... one he could lean against.

He gave my hand a squeeze, those dark eyes searching my face like I'd just given him the answer to the universe.

"Doc says she'll be okay. They're going to cast her, but I can take her home here shortly," Cal said, coming to stand in front of us. When he looked at mine and Jack's hands intertwined, he raised a brow.

I dropped Jack's hand, which he clearly didn't like.

"Fine," Jack said, and tugged on the cuff of his suit. "Once you leave with Bea, you want to set her up for the next couple weeks?"

Cal nodded. "Caribbean?"

"Or Arizona."

Caribbean? Arizona? They were either speaking in code words or their own special language. Or were they just taking a quick geography listing test?

"I'll see you in forty-eight hours," Cal said. Forty-eight hours? Cal must be going on shift at the station again. His schedule had to be all messed up with running in and out of work like he was.

"In the meantime, you're going to look into this company selling issue?"

Jack nodded.

"I still don't understand why my father's company is an issue."

"The sale of it is concerning," Jack started. "Since the meeting still stands, it is assumed his wife is taking over and continuing forward."

"Why is this so concerning?"

"Because money is involved. A lot of money. And people do stupid things for money."

"But my father's company, profits or otherwise, doesn't involve me," I said again. To which Jack crossed his arms.

"That we know of. But paperwork, legalities, and logistics tend to hide. I think you're more involved than you realize."

"How?"

He shook his head. "I don't know yet. But I have someone looking in to all of this."

Great. If things weren't crazy enough, another shadow of doubt got added to my father's company. Jack's logic made some sense. Brock had been looking for something in my house. Clearly one or both VanBurens didn't want me around. But why?

"So, your plan is that I stay in your house while this person you hired looks in to all of this?"

"My plan is to keep you safe until this issue in its entirety is resolved and you are no longer in danger."

"When is the sale of company supposed to happen?"

"In the afternoon of January second."

That was a few weeks away ... something I opened my mouth to say, but Jack cut me off before the first syllable came out.

"Don't attempt to argue with me. You're staying with me, for as long as it takes."

"I'm not yours to control," I said.

He crowded my space. "I'm looking for much more than control," he rasped, so only I could hear. "And deny it all you want, but you *are* mine, Lana. I recall you moaning that very admission while I was buried inside you."

My lips tingled and my body shot light like a freshly tapped snare drum. I was caught in his eyes, his dominating presence. All thoughts were routed to the one moment Jack had just painted in my mind. I had been his. Welcomed that thought. But that was the past.

"As you well know, control is something I enjoy, but in this circumstance, my main objective is your safety," he said, straightening his shoulders and moving away from me. His presence was hot, but with the few inches of distance, it was quickly cooling. And I wanted it back. So badly I wanted that heat back. How did he do that? Go from blood burning words to indifference in zero point two seconds?

He didn't fight fair, and my heart had the scars to prove it. Pressing my lips together, I tried to physically stop words, questions, anger, from coming out. Speech would only make things worse at this point. Because in the end, Jack was right. I'd done things my way, and Bea had gotten hurt. I couldn't argue. Didn't want to, because I cared about her. And, like it or not, the fire flared the fear that I'd been carrying this whole time. Someone was after me. And wasn't seeming to go away.

Jack moved beside me and rested his palm on my lower back. "Keep me posted," he said to Cal, then guided me down the hallway toward the exit. He was so close that his touch and scent enveloped my senses and reminded me of a time I'd gotten lost in both. Had been wrapped up in all that intensity that was radiating under his strong frame.

I glanced over my shoulder at Cal. He tossed me a wink and said, "I'll see you soon."

I nodded. Jack stopped for a beat, to throw his own look at Cal. The thoughts that radiated between the two of them were so palpable I could yank them out of the air.

And maybe Bea had been right. I was standing in the middle of two very strong, very alpha men, who both had no problem going after what they wanted.

In the time it took to get my measly bag of things from Cal's to Jack's house, he hadn't said a word to me, and I hadn't said a word to him either. What was I supposed to say? It was a car ride, and how did I broach the subject of the past months, about him leaving – all of it – in a handful of miles?

Truth was, I didn't know what Jack's response would be, and I didn't know if I'd want to hear it anyway.

It was done.

We were done.

Had been for a while.

Yet the void was pulsing like it was a living, breathing part of my body. I ignored it. Same as I had since he left.

He unlocked his front door and ushered me inside. I tugged the strap of my small bag that held a few items of clothing and toiletries I'd purchased since the fire, up on my shoulder. All I could afford at the moment, since everything had been burned.

"Would you like something to eat?" he asked.

"I just want to go to bed." After the accident with Bea, going to the hotel, and now back at Jack's, it had been a long day. It was getting dark, and while it may not be overly late, I was exhausted.

He looked at me for a long moment, then finally headed up stairs and I followed. I was determined to act as a guest. Like I hadn't crested these stairs several times. Like I hadn't been in Jack's arms one of the many times we'd climbed them. But I couldn't deny that the hardwood was a welcome sight, just like his scent and the warmth of his home.

When we reached the landing of the second floor, I saw the door to his bedroom down the hall and immediately turned the opposite direction, only to be hit with the sight of his office. The door was wide open, and I could see his desk. The massive centerpiece where I'd laid when he first tasted my body all those months ago.

Shivers broke over me. Staying here was a bad idea. But I couldn't argue safety anymore. And my choices were limited.

He took my bag off my shoulder in a quick, yet graceful maneuver, and walked towards his room.

"Ah, excuse me," I said, bounding after him. I didn't reach him until we were in the middle of his massive bedroom, the storm I'd once gotten caught up in. It looked exactly the same. Gray walls, white sheets on a bed that once was a cloud I lost myself in. The memory stung my eyes.

"I'd like my things back, and I'll be staying in the guest room," I informed him.

"You think so?" he said with a hint of amusement.

I took a deep breath and his scent engulfed me. He was standing before me. So close I could feel him, but I kept my eyes closed. Hoping that maybe he'd just fade away if I did.

"Interesting," he said, a single finger tracing my jawline. Not reacting to his touch was an impossibility. His touch affected me. And what was worse, he knew it. "Last time you were in this room, your eyes were open the whole time ... watching ... " His breath hit my ear. "Do you remember, baby? Remember how you clung to me?"

My eyes shot open and met his. Harnessing all the anger I could, I whispered, "I try to forget."

He stood to his full height and looked down at me as if assessing a challenge.

"We'll test your memory later," he said, then motioned toward his master bathroom. "You can shower in there if you'd like."

I did want a shower. Especially one with hot water.

Keeping my chin held up, I grabbed my bag back from him and headed into the bathroom. Although, after the stare down with Jack, a cold shower was sounding more necessary.

Chapter 7

The shower did little to calm my nerves. I couldn't deny the amazing scent of lavender shampoo. After taking time to scrub away the drama from the past couple weeks, I started feeling like a normal human again. I put the loofah back on the hook and ...

I ran my fingers over it once more.

The *pink* loofah.

Glancing around, I took a quick inventory of all the items in the shower. Everything from the soap to the conditioner was meant for a woman. That lavender shampoo I loved so much was actually my favorite. Just like the soap was.

I rinsed off quickly, stepped out, and wrapped a towel around me. Was this some elaborate plan? My one track mind was running on raw emotion as I marched out of the bathroom, bypassing the large open closet – I froze and looked in.

Shirts, sweaters, jeans and boots. All my size. All things I would pick out. He'd already bought them? No, no way was he doing this to me again.

I threw open the door that separated me from the master bedroom.

"You're unbelievable," I snapped.

He was already sitting in bed, as if sleep eluded him. Moonlight streamed in from the windows, making the gray walls look like a dancing rain cloud.

"Care to elaborate?" he said with sarcasm and stood. He was in black boxer briefs and all chiseled muscle and man. The way his abs flexed and his hips moved with every step toward me made my skin tighten and my mouth water. He was beautiful. Always had been. But with the soft white glow from the moon, his tanned skin held a sheen of silver. Like a god descending from a storm.

His dark eyes fixed on mine and I took a deep breath and forced composure . . . let my anger guide me. Oh, I'll elaborate alright.

"How dare you set me up again," I said, stepping further into his room.

"You mean, how dare I see to your needs?"

"This is still a game to you, isn't it? You knew I'd cave. Knew you'd get me to stay here. And you lined your closet and your bathroom with stuff for me?"

"Yes. And this is no game. It never was a game. How can I make you understand that?"

"Look at the closet and tell me how I'm supposed to think differently."

"You coming here, being with me, was a matter of time. Not some strategy."

I shook my head. Fury setting in. "You always have a plan, don't you?"

"No," he snapped. "There are times I'm caught off guard and have no fucking clue what to do. And even when I gain some kind of control, my best laid plans are shot to hell." He looked me dead in the eye. I was uncertain who was angrier. Because it was clear Jack was upset with me. Which only pissed me off more.

All the anger I'd saved up was coming to the surface. The one thing I'd been dying to do since he left, since I found out about the arrangement, was confront him.

"You say you care? Say you think of my safety? That I'm yours?" My chest heaved against the knot of my towel. "You left me. You had a deal with Cal, and both—"

"I don't want to talk about Cal," he said, continuing his slow stalk toward me.

"Good!" I shot back. "I don't either. I want to talk about *you*. How *you* think you can just tell me you care about me, tell me you believe me, then leave me. Now you're back thinking you can come in a save the day? Protect me? I'm not the person I once was."

"I know," he said with truth in his voice.

"I was fine," I said, warding off the brittle way the last word came out. "You came into my life. Now, I'm broken – no, not even broken. Broken would be a luxury I'd gladly take." One rogue tear fell, but I batted it away quickly, keeping my anger instead of sadness. "I'm empty."

He stopped. Both feet planted on the floor and I watched a deep, dark wave of emotion roll over his skin like lotion.

"I was so angry with you," he said so quietly I barely heard him. His black eyes burned with the very feeling he was describing.

He was angry with me? I was just about to ask him "what the hell" when his stillness was broken and he took another step toward me. His shoulders moved slow and graceful, like an animal ready to pounce.

"I wanted to kill that bastard that hurt you, that kept hurting you." His voice was jagged. "I *hated* that he'd stood in my office, right in front of me . . . " His fist clenched, but what was scarier was the single word he'd said that struck my chest hard.

Hate.

Jack hated that he'd conversed with Brock before knowing the kind of man he was. And I was the one who put Brock in front of him to begin with.

My chin started to quiver, but I folded my lips together to try to stop it. I didn't trust myself to speak. Didn't trust the anger I was clinging to because it was dissipating quickly and being replaced with more of that emptiness I was coming to recognize well.

Jack's eyes stayed right on my face. "Yes, Cal wanted time with you. I'd been prepared to fight him on that. To stay with you. But after seeing your step-brother, shaking his fucking hand and finding out what he'd done?" Jack shook his head. "I needed space to suppress the rage. It didn't take me long to realize that I hated the lack of control. Hated the situation. And it was because I love you so damn much."

I gasped, but his lips pulled back from his teeth and he bit the next words out.

"And I hated myself because I couldn't protect you." He closed in. Black gaze flaming from beneath thick lashes and said, "But, I can now. And I will. So, deal with it."

I swallowed hard, my head slowly turning from side to side, as if trying to register everything he'd just admitted. "You hated me?"

"Yes, because it was the only emotion I understood. I won't let anyone hurt you, Lana. Including yourself."

"That's not up to you," I whispered.

"Maybe not, but I won't stop trying."

"I hated you too," I admitted. "Still do. Because you ripped away everything when you left."

"You're strong, baby."

I didn't feel strong. I felt weak. Tired. Scared. Mad. So mad because he had the nerve to hate me . . . had even more nerve to love me.

"I'm sorry I met you," I said around clenched teeth.

He nodded and leaned closer, like he understood, was okay with me saying what I was saying. Which only heightened the bubbling anger to a full boil.

"I'm sorry I'm not as strong as you think." Keeping the tears pushed back was hard, but I did and powered through my thoughts. "I'm sorry I kept things from you. I'm sorry I thought I could handle it on my own. But, mostly, I'm sorry I fell in love with you."

He closed in on me and gripped the back of my head, threading his fingers through my hair. "That's a shame," he rasped and bit my lower lip. "Because I'm only sorry I left. And I'll be sorry for that for the rest of my life."

I pushed at his chest, but he didn't budge. Yet, somehow, pushing at him made me feel better. Made the anger rise and spew over like lava from a volcano. I got lost to it. Wanted to hurt him. Wanted him to feel the pain I was feeling. My palms slapped against his chest again, and again, he didn't budge. He let me hit him. Let me push at him. All while maneuvering me back against the wall. When he pressed me against it, his hand in my hair took the force so my head didn't hit. Even now, he was protecting me. And it only skyrocketed my anger.

The battery that was Jack Powell hummed with energy and gave me a full charge. He was trying to help me. Hold me.

I shoved at him again.

"Do what you need to do, baby," he growled in a thick deep voice. Those words broke past my consciousness and I did just that.

Do whatever it takes to get through this . . .

"You left me," I yelled and smacked his chest again.

"Yes," he admitted.

"You think I'm strong? Do I look like I'm strong to you?" I smacked again.

"You're the strongest person I've ever known," he said. "Stronger than me. Stronger than you realize."

I shook my head. It had taken everything I had to move away from his memory. And still, I wasn't over him. Would never be.

And it wasn't fair. The truth wasn't fair. The pain wasn't fair.

But life didn't care about fair.

"You. Left. Me!" Another slap, and he just took it.

My forehead fell against his bare chest, and I just heaved in and out oxygen. Waiting for this feeling to leave my system. My lips brushed against his skin and the slightest taste of him wasn't even close to enough. I was dipping my finger in the sugar bowl and wasn't ready to pull back. Instead, I took a deeper taste.

Parting my lips, I barely pushed my tongue enough to make contact with his smooth skin. He was hot and spicy and the tiniest hit of him sent an instant high racing through me.

His free hand came up to cup my throat and I looked him in the eye . . . our mouths open and a fraction apart, breathing each other in.

"I'm sorry," he said.

"I'm sorry too," I admitted. "But part of me still hates you."

"Good," he grinned. "Because that means you still love me."

Logic was gone. Emotions took over. I crushed my mouth against his. My hands against his chest turned to nails and scraped down his torso. All those cut abdominal muscles jumped beneath my touch and skyrocketed me over the edge. I knew this man. Knew him so well it was slowly killing me how much I

72

loved him. Missed him. Recognized him. Every inch of his skin, every brush of his hands, my body registered like he was its master. And I was helpless against it.

"Nothing is more important to me than you," he said against my mouth. He kissed me hard. Deep. Plunging his tongue to ravage my mouth and eat up my taste like a ravenous man with his last meal.

Tugging at my towel, he threw it open and it fell to the floor. The instant my skin met his was like coming home. My breasts pressed against his hot torso, making breathing impossible in the best way.

He grabbed my hips, his thumbs digging in, and slid them up my sides to my ribs. "Fuck I've missed you. Miss this perfect curve. Missed your sweet taste." His hands were everywhere. Seeking out my skin roughly, like his fingertips were starved for a drink.

I threaded my fingers through his hair and bit down on his bottom lip. He hissed and shoved his tongue deeper. Pressing me further into the wall, he kicked my legs apart and hoisted me up. With a single arm wrapped around my waist, I locked my legs behind his back and kept kissing him. Hard and fast. Our teeth banged against each other's. I paused only to scrape them against his jaw, then back to his mouth, as I went in for another brutally penetrating kiss.

Jack was a man who was always in control. But, right then, he was as lost as I was. I could feel it. Feel him. The part of my soul he'd taken with him was, for a moment, sparking to life.

"I've missed my woman," he said, reaching between us to shove down his boxers. He used the head of his cock to find my slick heat. "Tell me you've missed me."

"I have." I cupped his face and kissed the side of his mouth, his cheekbone.

He ran the velvety crown between my folds, hitting the sensitive bundle of nerves, making me gasp.

"Tell me what you want."

"You," I said around a moan. He was grinding, up and down, against my damp core and it was driving me to the brink of blissful agony.

"Say it again," he rasped against my face.

"I want you, Jack."

I barely got his name past my lips when the thick head of his shaft breached me and he surged deep.

"Oh, God!" I screamed out. He groaned as he withdrew a few inches, then thrust up, impaling me again.

"Fuck, baby," he said, like he was in pain, or ecstasy. But feeling him deep inside me turned everything I'd been fighting up a notch, and I lost myself to him. To missing him. To hating him. To loving him. Just lost everything.

"More," I told him. Begged him. More of all of it. Because I couldn't handle thinking. Couldn't handle real life or what any of this meant. Couldn't handle the past or the future. I just wanted to get through this. And that's what I was doing.

He thrust in and out. My ass hitting the wall while he fucked me with all his strength. I held on to him, my nails digging into his back as I kissed him over and over until it wasn't kissing anymore. It was tasting, biting, devouring. There was nothing sweet. Nothing slow. Nothing sensual about it. His skin slickened with sweat as he pumped harder, deeper, taking everything I had left to give, which I hadn't even known existed. But Jack somehow found the last ounce of hope, the last fraction of the soul I had left, and tapped into it. Took me to the edge while I screamed his name and begged him not to stop.

"Look at me," he said, one hand coming up to cup my face.

I squeezed my eyes shut. Purposefully disobeying him. Partly because I couldn't let him think he had control, couldn't give in that easily. And partly because I was terrified of what I'd see in his eyes.

He thrust so hard, I squeaked with pleasure. He hit the end of every nerve I had.

"Look. At. Me," he demanded.

I squeezed my eyes shut tighter. I was afraid. So afraid of the cliff I was about to fall over that I couldn't bear to look at his perfect face. Couldn't risk what I'd see staring back at me because, better or worse, it would be my undoing.

He pumped faster. The sound of him working my body over, thudding against the wall only heightened my lust. Pressing further against me, he ground his hips so there wasn't an inch between us. He had me pinned. Unmovable. My body stuck between a wall and him, his hard muscles and hard cock the only leverage I had. And he wasn't letting me go. Wasn't pulling back, not even an inch.

"Stubborn woman," he said, gripping me tight and stuffing that massive shaft into me over and over until my legs went limp. But he was so close that my thighs bobbed around his sides, unable to do anything but remain parted for him.

God, I loved it. Totally taken over, past the point of want and need. He was my air. The single thing I needed to breathe right.

Deep. He was so deep and only growing harder. My inner walls flooded with heat and a slow, hot lust clawed at my spine and shot out to the tips of my fingers and toes, burning up everything in its path. I clawed his back. Holding on for dear life. I'd never felt anything like the kind of release my body was pushing itself through. It was rolling over me in waves, gradually picking up pace while sticking me with shards of bright pleasure.

I was coming, yet still on the brink. The intensity rising while I was already in a free fall. I felt him right there with me, ready to jump over the edge.

"Please, baby . . . " he whispered in my ear and the sound of his voice, a voice that was so stern, so certain all the time, held a tremor of begging. It stabbed at my chest like a rusty blade. "Please, look at me."

I couldn't bear the sound of this strong man so wounded.

I opened my eyes and looked into the dark obsidian depths of his. Relief washed over him and he held me . . . kept that wild loving gaze fastened to mine as he came apart.

Bright light snapped through my veins like a drug. I opened my mouth to scream, but no words came out. Just a gasp as my body lit up with sparks of pleasure, of pain. It was so intense that it sizzled like a hot stone dropped into glacier water. He held me tight as it took us both over. And I did what I'd always done in this room. I clung to him.

Buried deep and gaze fastened to mine, he watched as every wave of ecstasy came over my face and only when I was on the brink of coming down, I felt his release. So powerful it made my entire body shudder and flick my orgasm into another few seconds of overdrive.

"My Lana," he whispered against my face and kissed me softly on the lips. "Mine."

I was stuck there, between the wall and the man I loved, still loved, and hated all at the same time, and had no idea how to feel.

But something odd poked from within my chest. On a heavy inhale, I realized it was my heart . . . starting to beat again.

Chapter 8

The last couple of days had passed in a blur. After hurling myself over the brink of sanity with Jack, I'd spent most of my time in the guest room. I couldn't shake the extreme exhaustion following me around. My body was off kilter, but after two days and random bouts of sleeping, I was feeling more rested, but more confused.

The other night, I'd gone to Jack with anger, looking for closure, and now I was more lost than ever. The awful part was, I was less hollow. Being with him had actually pulled the strings holding the broken pieces inside me together. What passed between us melded onto my shattered soul and started the slightest process of healing. But that couldn't be right. There was too much still to sift through. Too much damaged trust.

And Cal.

I loved Cal. That hadn't changed. I also wasn't with Cal, since he was a part of this whole mess from the beginning. My entire body was pulled in opposites directions. And I had no idea where to turn.

Jack hadn't approached me. He stayed mostly in his office and let me live out the day in my self-imposed cave, leaving a tray of food outside the door. I wondered if I could hide in the dark corner of this room for the rest of my life—

The thought sank in and hurt to repeat out loud.

"Dark corner," I whispered to myself, since no one could hear. Jack was my dark corner. Where I hid from the world and he wrapped me up and let me. And that's what I was doing. Hiding. Something Cal would never allow.

I ran both hands through my hair and wanted to scream. That pulling that was happening? Was getting worse.

I looked out the window and paced the room for the millionth time. When a truck pulled up, I glanced out to see Cal walking up and coming inside. It wasn't long before his heavy boots passed my room and headed toward Jack's office. Their muffled voices rang out and I decided that I had to stop hiding.

Straightening my shirt and running my palms down my jeans, I walked out and toward Jack's office. Both men froze mid-sentence when I entered.

"How's Bea?" I asked.

Cal faced me. He looked so tired, and even though he was stacked with large muscles, his eyes were sunken in like he hadn't slept in days.

"She's doing well. Small fracture, but she's okay. She's on a cruise with her friend for a few weeks."

"Caribbean?" I asked, their secret lingo now making a bit more sense.

He nodded. They were getting Bea away so she couldn't be in danger. Sweet boys. I chanced a glance at Jack. Mistake. He was sitting behind his desk, eyes focused on me. Cal seemed to notice the exchange, but didn't say anything.

"Tell her," Jack said to Cal.

Cal looked at me and scratched the back of his head. "I've

been looking into your dad's life and company from before he died."

This again? Sure, I could suspend my thoughts enough to think perhaps something was amiss. But it was likely just Anita and Brock worried I'd fight them for my dad's money. There were no documents supporting this, though.

"I told you, I'm not in the will."

"I know," Cal said. "But that has nothing to do with it. Someone thinks you're a threat in some way, otherwise, this shit wouldn't keep happening." I recognized that anger in his voice. Cal got mad whenever someone he loved was in danger. While Jack harnessed his control in other ways, Cal found his in physically protecting those around him. My heart beat an extra time at that notion.

"A lot of documents and contracts go between companies that have nothing to do with wills. We're finding out more about the timeline, though, and it's too coincidental to ignore," Jack added.

"What are you talking about?" I asked.

"We know your father was set to sell, and the process is still underway. But when he decided to sell is odd. He reached out for offers right before Brock came back to Denver," Jack clarified.

"So, I did some digging," Cal said. "I went to talk to your mom."

"You what? Why would you do that?" I hadn't spoken to my mother in a long time.

"Because she's the only one who could have information about the time before your dad met Anita and the company went from Case to Case-VanBuren."

My mouth went dry. Cal hadn't been at the station, he'd been traveling. My mother was the only one who could possibly have any information.

"Did she say anything?" I asked.

Cal nodded. "She gave me the name of your father's attorney and accountant, same man who handled all his business and financial work when they were still married. He's in Denver. We can go see him when his office opens tomorrow."

"I don't know if there is any information to be had, though."

Cal shrugged. "It's better than sitting here doing nothing and waiting for someone to hurt you." He pulled a small envelope from the inside of his jacket pocket. "She also gave me this."

He handed it to me and inside were a few small photos of when I was a child. One was of my father and me. The others were of all three of us. A family.

Water lined my eyes and I looked at Cal. "How did you know I wanted this?"

He moved toward me, not reaching out, but enough to put our bodies so close that I could feel his torso rise and fall against my breasts with each breath he took. "The night Harper was at the house, she called me after you talked and told me."

I searched his face, now realizing that he was likely tired because he'd spent the last day and a half on an airplane or talking to my mother.

His hand cupped my waist, pulling me just a little closer, and I let him. Liking the feel of his strength against me. Liking the way he towered over me and made me feel safe and warm and cherished.

"I told you, Kitten. All you have to do is tell me what you need, and I'll make it happen."

I met his eyes. Blue and bright and laced with sadness. I glanced over his shoulder and saw Jack starring daggers in our direction.

80

Cal's shoulders stiffened, just before they sunk just slightly. He moved away from me and spared Jack a single glance before returning that ocean gaze back on me, full heat ignited.

"But maybe I was wrong about what you needed," Cal rasped with a harsh bite.

My breath caught and I clutched the pictures he'd given me. Looking between the man that delivered and the man that conquered, I was at a loss for what to say. What to feel. Because what I felt for each of them was very different, yet very deep.

As if Cal could read my mind, he shot me a heated look and a devastating grin. "If there is one thing I've learned, it's that timing is everything." He walked past me and out of Jack's office. As he stomped down the hallway, he called over his shoulder, "I'm going to get my bag from the truck. Hope you don't mind one more crashing at your place, Jack."

With that, the strong firefighter strode down the hall and out of sight, leaving me, if possible, even more at odds with everything.

"We need to talk," Jack said immediately. His voice rolled over my skin and pricked it with shivers.

I turned to face him. "I think we've said everything we need to."

"I disagree completely." He stood from behind his desk. His light blue button up was the color of Cal's eyes and rolled at the sleeves. But the powdery color made his dark features stand out like an exotic treat.

"I was looking for closure," I admitted, hoping to get out of this room and conversation without Jack hearing my heart pick up its pace.

"Oh?" he asked, rounding his desk and heading my way. The man didn't walk. He stalked. Like a predator. And, once again, like the moment I met him, I felt the trance of his intensity sweep me up. "And is that what you got? Closure?"

I licked my lips and tried to stand tall, tried to keep eye contact and not show weakness, but his eyes were so smoldering it was hard not to get hit with the heat.

"Yes," I said, softer than I'd meant to.

A sexy grin tugged his face, that strong jaw working over a five-o'clock shadow that made me recall every scrape and feel of it against my skin.

"You never were a good liar," he said. "In fact, I think the opposite happened. I think instead of closure . . . " he trailed his hand up my inner thigh, "You opened up a little more to me."

Tremors skated over my body. The anger had ebbed since the other night, but reality hadn't. The truth remained. He left, lied, and broke a piece of me I'd never be able to repair.

"I've thought of you every day. Every moment of *every damn day*," he rasped.

"And were you counting down the clock until it was your turn to make a go at me again?"

"It was never like that. You know it. Deep down, you know how I feel about you."

"How you feel about me?" I asked and took a step back. "Is that the feeling that made you leave, compelled you to stay gone, and show up only when I'd fallen in love with Cal?"

His jaw clenched. But Jack opened this can of worms.

"Oh, you don't like that?" I asked. "Me saying the truth? That I fell in love with Cal? That while you were thinking of me, I was thinking of him. Maybe you should have *thought* of that before making the arrangement you did."

"Say it then, Lana. Tell me you didn't think of me. Tell me you don't still. Tell me we're done."

His voice was so even it was chilling. Jack Powell was either the world's best bluffer or just dared me to walk away. Problem was, I couldn't. He was pushing, and all I could do was push back. Just like he'd taught me.

"I'm done with this conversation," I said.

Jack smiled. "Ah, that's a win in my book, baby." And he was right. I couldn't tell him I was done with him, because honestly, maybe I never would be. I loved the prick. Loved him so much I hated him for it.

But I loved Cal. So much it tore every time I took a breath.

I couldn't fall into the pattern of what it felt like to be with either of them. Because not only was neither of them an option, but my world couldn't handle another quake.

"This is going to get more difficult before it gets easier," Jack said, as if he too had some direct line to my thoughts.

Of that, I totally believed him.

Chapter 9

It was past ten at night, and I hadn't risked another conversation with either Cal or Jack since I'd left his office earlier. Instead, I'd been attempting to keep myself busy by pretending to concentrate on my thesis project.

The second-hand laptop I'd gotten was barely working, but it had enough juice to check my email and type. With school being out for winter and my proposal with the thesis board, there wasn't much I could do until the new term started. But that didn't stop me from trying to focus on anything other than my current situation.

I crisscrossed my legs on my bed and scrolled through my inbox. I was surprised to see an email from Erica.

Opening it, I read her message. She was safe, staying with her mother and looking at extending her sabbatical or finding a new job far away from Denver. Her daughter was doing well and the more I read her words, the better I felt about the decision to let the break-in rest. I couldn't drag her back here to testify against Brock. I also wouldn't risk her safety or her daughter's. The best thing for them was to stay far away from Brock ... and from me. Starting a new life was best.

With a deep breath, I closed my email. At least someone had closure. And I was happy Erica and her daughter could move on.

Stretching my arms overhead, I quickly searched the Internet in hopes for a further distraction, since thoughts of Jack's touch and Cal's kiss were starting to creep back in.

Tomorrow, we'd go see the attorney. See if there was any information I could get about my dad, because Jack and Cal were right, something had to be going on. Even though right now there was no hard evidence to support the theory of me being a threat of any kind to my father's estate or money, it was something worth asking questions about.

The Internet was little help. I tried researching my father, a man and his company I should already know about. All I got were stats and Wikipedia answers. I went through the stock market and it appeared that the Case-VanBuren stock had taken a hit over the past two quarters, which was news to me. I knew the business had needed some new clients, hence the mess I'd gotten into with Jack, but the stock was hurting more than I'd realized. A reason my father was looking to sell, maybe?

A light knock came at my bedroom door. I shut the laptop. "Yes?"

The knob turned slowly. It could be one of two men and I held my breath, wondering which one it would be.

As the door swung wide, Cal stood, in all his masculine glory, sweaty, shirtless and in nothing but a pair of low-slung shorts. He held a box in one hand and waited on the other side of the threshold.

"Hey," I said, licking my lips and trying not to stare at his defined chest and amazing tattoos. "Just get done exercising?" It was a stupid question. Between the sheen of sweat and heavy breaths of his chest, he appeared to have come straight to my room after whatever kind of workout he'd just finished.

His blue eyes landed on mine and he nodded. "Yeah, exercising isn't what it used to be."

The statement hit my chest and spread over my skin like warm water. Because that single statement brought back some potent memories. Like the time I'd been with him at the fire house. Straddling his lap while he lifted weights. Stealing kisses between reps. My entire body ached from the recollection.

"Can I come in?" he asked.

It would be smart to say no. To tell him distance was best. Instead, I nodded. Smart didn't outweigh the want to be near him.

He took a few long strides and didn't stop until he was sitting on the edge of the bed. His scent was intoxicating. Spicy and woodsy and all man. I wanted to taste every inch of his salty skin and do a different kind of marathon, but that was not where we were anymore. The light and fun time in our relationship had passed. We didn't even have a relationship anymore. And that fact knocked on something already broken deep in my chest.

"I see you're still hiding out in here," he said, setting the box on the bed next to me.

"I'm not hiding."

He grinned. "You're not a good liar, Kitten."

Second man to say that to me today. Not cool.

"Did you want something?"

"Yes," he said with a serious edge. "I want something very much actually." Those aqua eyes bore into mine and just the intensity from his stare made my blood heat.

"Cal . . ." I whispered. Which made him close his eyes for a moment and take a deep breath, as if warding off some kind of pain.

"Do you have any idea how hard it is to hear you say my name, be close to you, and know you're so far away?"

There was rawness behind every syllable. "Yes," I answered honestly. "I know exactly how that feels."

"Then, tell me," he asked. "Tell me everything. Be mad, say whatever you need to say. Please, I'm right here and I want to hear it. Whatever needs to happen so we can—"

"Move on?" I interrupted.

"Yes," he whispered. "Move on."

"Funny thing about that," I said around a shuddering voice. "There are some things that are impossible to move on from." He hung his head and our conversation from all those weeks ago hit hard. "You were the one who told me that moving on from something that causes so much joy or pain is impossible."

"So, move then, Kitten. Please, just move toward me."

"I don't think I can." The truth punched my stomach so hard it made me want to retch.

"Then, do something, make me pay, anything."

I shook my head and did the one thing I tried from the beginning to never do, I reached out for him. Cupping his face in my hands, I stared at the man I loved so much, but couldn't have. "I don't want to be mad anymore."

"No," he said sternly. "Give me anger. Hate. Anything. But don't give up on us."

I looked at the big strong man before me and realized how different he was. In every way. Not just from Jack, but from all men. Jack had my anger, even some hate, and he thrived on it. There was hope in it. Jack knew it. And so did Cal.

How and what I felt for Cal was complex. Not better or worse – if there was such a thing.

"What I feel for you isn't vicious. It's . . . devastating."

He looked like I'd just punched him in the face. "No," he said again, his male dominance rising to the surface. "No, Lana. I fucked up. But that doesn't mean what we have isn't real. I love you, God damn it."

I swallowed hard and he leaned in closer. I went to pull my hand away, but he clasped it against his face.

"Look at me right now and tell me to leave you alone. Tell me you're through with me."

It sounded so similar to what Jack had asked. If I was done, I needed to say so now. All the strength in the world didn't match my greatest weakness. Which was them. Both of them.

I couldn't bring the word to my lips. Because, just like I'd faced down Jack's question, I faced Cal's. And I couldn't deny the truth. I did want him. So much. And it was tearing me up inside.

"It's hard enough to deal with what happened between us, but Jack too? I . . . I don't know where to start."

"Start here." Using his free hand he pushed the box closer to me. "There's no pressure. I'm not going anywhere. I don't give a shit what it takes or how long, you're mine," he said, and kissed my inner wrist. "When you're done hiding, you know I'll always chase you."

With that, he rose and walked out the door, shutting it softly behind him. I sat there, stunned. Cal's approach was calm, but his dominance was very clear. He made his claim just like Jack had. And at one point, I'd given myself to each of them. I just never thought either of our relationships would end up like this.

I looked at the box he'd just left and opened it.

It was a pair of running shoes.

My strong alpha warrior challenged me, told me what I was capable of, told me what he was willing to do, and left it up to me. Like he always did.

I clutched the box to my chest, the piece of my heart that belonged to Cal throbbing with every beat.

Chapter 10

I'd given in and raided the closet in Jack's room after he left for work this morning. Not because I wanted to, but because meeting with my father's old attorney was nerve-racking enough and the plain T-shirts I had wouldn't cut it. I wanted to look somewhat decent.

Somehow, the guys had worked out for one of them to always be with me. How they kept their schedules, I didn't know. And I wouldn't ask, since their constant presence was hindering my plan for distance.

A pair of dark jeans and a fuzzy pink sweater later – coupled with some make up and an amazing shower – I looked almost like myself again. Something Cal took an extra-long glace at as he held the office door open that led to Henry Dwyer, Attorney at Law.

When I stepped through, his hand rested on the small of my back. The warmth that came from him was encompassing. It took a lot of concentration to be around either of them. A single glance or quick touch and I forgot the past and got lost in Jack's dark eyes or Cal's dimpled smile.

Cal sat in the small waiting area as the secretary ushered me through one more door.

"Mr. Dwyer, Lana Case to see you." The woman smiled and left us.

"Hello," he said in a cheery voice and shook my hand.

"Thank you for meeting with me on such short notice," I said.

"Of course." He gestured for me to sit and I did. "After I got your call, I looked through all my old files. I put it . . . " He got up and walked to the large cabinet in the corner.

He was sweet, but the deep wrinkles in his forehead and thin, combed-over white hair, told me he had to be pushing seventy. I sat in the squeaking chair while he fumbled through his massive file cabinet, pausing only to shove the thick-brimmed glasses up his nose.

I glanced behind me at the "Henry Dwyer, Attorney at Law" on the window and knew Cal was on the other side of the door, waiting for me.

"I haven't seen Carter Case in years," Henry said, looking through more files. "We ended our contract a while ago. He had a great mind for business." He dug in the back and came up with a manila envelope. "Ah! Here it is."

He came to sit behind his desk once more, a bit winded, and opened the envelope. A single piece of paper came out, with what looked to be a key taped to it.

"I am really sorry to hear of his passing," Henry said, looking at me.

"Thank you."

He read over the single sheet of paper then handed it to me. "This belongs to you. I don't know what the key goes to, but the document is notarized."

I frowned. It was a short document that said the contents of the corresponding box that matches this key goes to Lana Case. And it was executed right after my father married Anita.

"Thank you so much," I said. He stood and shook my hand and I felt a little lighter. Maybe this would help solve the apprehension behind everything going on. At one point, my father had thought of me. Thought of the future. And this key was ... the key.

Leaving the office, I saw Cal in the waiting room, flipping through some car magazine, then standing when he saw me.

"Got what you needed?"

"I have no idea," I answered honestly. As we walked out to his truck, the sun was fading into purples. He opened the truck door and helped me in.

"It's a key, but I don't know to what."

Cal glanced at it and started the engine. "It's small. Some kind of lockbox? A safe maybe?"

I shrugged. "It's from roughly ten years ago, so I have no idea. If he had a safe, Anita would have found it by now."

"It may not be a safe then. We can do some research."

I smiled at him. The term "we" made my body feel less heavy, and it was another one of those split seconds I forgot the real world. With a deep breath, the despair came back as realization of the last week hit home.

Could I ever move on from Cal? From Jack?

No.

I knew that to be true. The question was, how do I survive in the meantime?

Cal's phone pinged. He grabbed it out of his pocket and read a text. "Jack is done in an hour and will meet us at home."

Meet us at home? This wasn't some sleepover party. While the idea sounded amazing for the simplest of seconds, this wasn't a situation that I'd say was conventional, nor was Jack's home my home.

I didn't have a home, actually.

But family? Friends? All of that was scattered few and far between, leaving me longing for the word home while being sucker-punched with the reality that even if I had a roof of my own, there was no one to fill it with.

I looked at Cal. So familiar, riding in his truck, his tattoos peeked out from beneath his T-shirt sleeve. A couple weeks ago we would have gone to his home, he would have made me feel like I belonged there, and I'd kiss every inch of ink he had. But this wasn't a couple weeks ago.

"Smile for me, Kitten."

"What?" I asked.

He glanced at me when we turned down Jack's street. "I can't handle you looking at me like that."

Whatever look I was giving wasn't a good one, and I didn't want Cal thinking I was a wreck. Even though I was. Call it pride or stupidity, but I was trying to at least give the impression that I could somehow manage being a functioning human. So far, it was challenging.

"Remember when you were at Bea's with me and she brought out the scrapbooks?"

I smiled, even laughed a little recalling the memory. "Yeah, page after page of naked baby pictures."

He looked at me and smiled back. He'd gotten what he wanted. What he'd asked of me. A smile.

But his expression turned serious quickly when we pulled up to Jack's and saw the window smashed, the door busted open, and the alarm going off.

"Stay here," Cal said.

The blaring noise from the security system was screaming and shards of glass picking up flecks of light were shimmering in the grass.

"Wait, no!"

"The police are dispatched as soon as the alarm goes off. They're not here yet, which means it just happened and the asshole is still inside," he said, as he got out of the truck and headed toward the house.

"Cal, stop!" But he was already bounding through the front door.

A loud thud, then glass breaking shot over the alarm, and I jerked the door open. Cal was in there. I screamed his name again when more crashing noises came.

I barely made it three steps before Cal ran out the front of the house and looked both ways.

"Mother fucker!" he cursed, then ran toward me. "I'm getting you out of here now." He ambled me back into the truck. For a second, I thought he was going to hoist me over his shoulder. Instead, his big body just overtook mine as he maneuvered me like a doll into the vehicle and shut the door. He was around the front and behind the wheel peeling away in record time.

"Cal, what happened? Are you okay?"

"Slippery fucker got out. I didn't know if he was coming for you."

"Are you okay?" I asked again. My heart was jumping in my throat and banging so loud it was hard to hear over the rushing in my eardrums.

"I'm fine. Just need to get you away from here." He made several turns until we were bounding down a back dirt road. The sound of sirens in the distance echoed.

A flare of red marked his forehead. I reached over to touch his chin and tilt him slightly toward me.

"Oh, my God, you're bleeding."

He frowned, then looked in the rearview mirror.

"It's fine. Just a scrape."

"No, it's not fine." I unbuckled my seatbelt and he pulled to the side of the dark road.

"Put your belt back on."

"Not until I look at this," I said, moving closer to him. He killed the engine and I unbuckled him and cupped his face in both hands. The same fire I'd felt when Bea got hurt shot through me. There was a cut on the top of his brow, right by his hair line.

"I'm fine," he said again.

"Will you shut up?" I said and took the sleeve of my sweater and blotted at the blood, clearing it away. Thank God it wasn't deep. But, he'd been in there, running toward a danger without even thinking. "What is the matter with you?" I yelled at him. "You can't keep doing this, Cal. You can't run in after every damn scary situation and leave me like that. You could have been hurt. You *were* hurt!"

He smiled.

"This isn't funny!" I yelled louder. My pulse was working double-time and my palms trembled. "You can't do that to me."

"Careful, Kitten, you may admit you care."

I frowned, and an anvil to the chest would have rocked me less. "I *do* care. So much. If anything happened to you ... I ... I love you, you big jerk!"

He closed his eyes and lifted his head up slightly, like he would if enjoying the warmth of the sun of his face.

"You love me," he repeated softly around a happy smile.

I tapped his cheek and his eyes opened and centered on me. "This is serious."

"Oh, I know it is," he winked. His hands slid around my waist and I moved across his lap and straddled it like it was most natural thing in the world.

"I will always protect you," he said, touching my forehead with his.

I inhaled deeply, the only breath I needed was Callum Malone. Between the worry, the adrenaline, and the softness of his voice, I couldn't fight it anymore. Part of me wanted to continue yelling at him, but a bigger part just wanted him. In my arms, wrapped around me, until I lost myself completely.

His nose brushed mine, his mouth so close I could almost taste it. The grip on my waist moved to my ass and tightened, but he didn't draw me close. Just sat there, waiting for me to come to him.

"Don't do that again," I whispered.

He gave my bottom a squeeze. "Which part?"

"The running into danger part."

"Can't promise that," he rasped lowly, brushing the tip of his nose along my cheek, daring me to kiss him. "It's the way I'm wired."

"Then I'll run in after you." He leaned back an inch to look me in the eye. "Because that's the way I'm wired."

I pressed my lips against his, giving in to the need we were circling. A dam burst, and feeling his strength surround me, I clutched him closer and surged my tongue inside, drinking in everything he'd give me.

He met my mouth with consuming force and returned every sweep and drive, tangling so tightly until neither of us could think. Could breathe.

I moaned and was swept up in his incredible kiss. He was a protector down to his soul.

Cal just ran into the fray without a thought other than to keep me safe. And I could have lost him. Had almost lost him on more than one occasion.

Just the idea had me near tears. I wrapped my arms around his neck and hugged him close, kissing him with all the strength I had.

I was frantic. The need to touch him – feel him – overwhelming. I ran my hands beneath his shirt and up his abs. All his hard muscles jerked and flexed against my touch, as if his body missed me as much as I missed his.

He met every single lick and bite I delivered. Dueling with my tongue and demanding more. He caged me to his hard body, pressing me so close my breasts mashed against his chest and begged for more direct contact.

Taking long laps of his intoxicating taste like he was my last glass of water before the desert, I rocked against him, rubbing the swollen peaks of my breasts up and down his chest.

"My kitten wants to be pet," he rasped, and sucked the tip of my tongue before leaning back enough to tug my sweater up. But before he could, his cellphone chirped, snapping my attention back to the present.

The chirping sounded again and Cal cursed. He reached for his cell out of his pocket and hit the answer button.

"Where the hell are you?" Jack's voice came over the speaker.

"There was a break-in at your place," Cal answered.

"No shit. I got a call. I'm at the house. Where. The hell. Are *you*?"

"Cops weren't there yet. Someone was still inside. I got Lana out of there."

"Is she okay?"

Cal's eyes met mine and he grinned. "She's doing pretty well from what I can tell."

I huffed out a breath.

Jack was silent.

I realized right then that this was turning into a different kind of game. Bea's words bounced into my mind. Nothing had ever come between Jack and Cal . . . except me. And at the moment, it was almost literal.

Just like Cal had known the other day what had happened between Jack and me, Jack seemed to know – judging by his silence – what had happened between Cal and me just now.

I moved off of Cal's lap and sat back in my own seat.

After a long pause, Jack spoke again.

"I'm taking her away."

"Like hell you are," Cal said. "And to where? A high rise hotel where anyone can come and go?"

"She's not going to your house. That's too obvious," Jack growled.

"Then, the cabin," Cal shot out quickly, like an epiphany had hit him.

Another long pause and Jack's even breathing passed over the phone for several seconds. Thinking. Jack always thought through every detail.

"Fine. I'll get stuff for all of us packed up. Meet me at the cabin. I'm done with this bullshit."

"Ten four, good buddy," Cal said, and hung up.

Cal looked over at me just as I got my seatbelt on.

"Don't look so victorious," I said.

He reached over and ran his thumb along my bottom lip, then tasted it. "Sorry, just feeling on top of the world right now. That happens when you come in and rock it, Kitten."

Normally, Cal's confident casualness made me feel better. This time, I was on the brink of a tough conversation while heading into a warzone. Cal was on one side, Jack was on the other, and I stood dead center, a pile of grenades surrounding me.

This was bad.

My emotions, anger, and love for them had just stuck me in a spot I didn't know how to get out of.

"It's alright," Cal said with gentleness. "You'll like the cabin."

That's what I was afraid of. That and being in this mystery cabin with two men I'd recently slept with.

With a final look at me, Cal started the truck, and turned back toward the highway, speeding to an unknown destination in the night.

Chapter 11

After a long drive, we made it to a single road covered in snow that led us through acres of trees until, finally, a small house came into view.

A black Jeep was parked out front.

"Looks like Jack beat us here," Cal said. I'd never seen Jack drive a Jeep, but it made sense he'd need that kind of car with the snow and terrain around here.

After helping me out of the truck, Cal opened the front door, and I walked in. The warmth and smell of trees was strong and welcoming. More welcoming than the dark eyes staring me down from the living room. I glanced away from Jack and his questioning stare and tried to focus on the place.

The cabin was beautiful. Secluded deep in the mountains of the Rockies, it was cozy with wood furniture and red accents. The snow lightly falling outside like pieces of fluffy cotton was picturesque. Or it could have been if I wasn't standing between two hulking men glaring each other down.

Three large bags lay by the front door, where Jack had clearly dropped them.

"Whose place is this?" I asked, trying to break the silence.

"Ours," Cal answered, and lifted his chin at Jack. "Bought it together several years ago. Nice escape."

"You'll be safe," Jack said, his dark eyes zeroing in on Cal, but he was talking to me.

"What about your jobs?" I asked, glancing between them. I hadn't wanted to pry, but this set up, far out as we were, seemed like a lot of time to take out of their lives.

"I own my company," Jack said simply. Aka, he could do whatever he wanted. Should have known.

Cal just smiled and tossed an arm around my shoulders. "Vacation time is saved up. Decided I better start using some of it."

Jack eyed Cal's arm like it was a snake around me. I couldn't take the tension. Between the two of them, it was suffocating. Life was spiraling, yet for the first time, the confusion wasn't daunting. Being with Jack and Cal and coming to some kind of conclusion had helped. Sure, having sex with both of them was what put me in the situation, but it was something that needed working out. I was just happy the emptiness and loss were starting to ebb, even in the smallest amount.

Doing what I have to do to get through this . . .

I stepped away from Cal, but made sure to stay in neutral territory and not lean toward Jack either.

"Clearly, we need to address what's going on and what has happened," I said.

Jack looked at me. "I think that's a great idea. Let's start with what happened the other night in my bedroom." His voice was smooth and clear and held that hint of confidence that was Jack Powell through and through. Just the way he reigned his calm control over every syllable made me jolt with lust.

Getting lost in him was easy. So damn easy, and giving myself over to whatever he wanted was even easier. Something I needed to fight, because with the emotions rising, the emotions he brought out in me couldn't have a voice. I needed to figure out me.

"I don't think we need details," Cal said. "Unless you'd like to share about our exciting ride up here tonight." He winked at me.

Jack's face remained still.

"Nope," I said and moved to face them both. "If you two want to give each other hell, fine. But I'm taking myself out of the middle. Things between all of us need to get resolved on some level." On a deep breath, I started the conversation I'd dreaded the entire trip up here. "I've had intimate moments with both of you." No matter how I tried to spin the next part, I couldn't be sorry for that.

I wasn't looking to make problems, I'd given in to very strong, very deep feelings I had for them and allowed them to take over. And those brief moments I couldn't be sorry for. Because while this was a mess, it wasn't a mistake. I loved them and in our private moments, I got to feel that love. Even if it was fleeting.

"I'm aware you've been with both of us," Jack said. Cal nodded in agreement.

"I know this isn't a surprise to you. But I wanted to put it out in the open. It's the only way to move on from it."

"Agreed," Cal said. "Though I don't think moving on from *every moment* is necessary." He was clearly referring to our time being something to hold on to. "But since we're stuck here for the next couple weeks—"

"We should come up with some ground rules," Jack cut in.

"Wait, we're here until the New Year?" I asked. Christmas was right around the corner. Not that I had anyone to spend it with,

102

but I had things to do. At some point, I'd wanted to find a job, but first, "I need to find what that key of my father's goes to."

"What key?"

I pulled the key and note out of my pocket and showed Jack. He read it quickly, then examined the key.

"I can tell you right now it's a lockbox," Jack said.

"How do you know?"

He just looked at me with the expression that read, "Don't you know who I am?"

"I know what lockbox keys look like. I have several. We just have to figure out which bank. With the holidays, the banks will be closed frequently. Calling around is the best use of time until after the New Year."

I gritted my teeth. Part of me hated him telling me the plan. Not asking, telling. The other part of me responded so quickly and wanted to say, "yes, sir," because he was right. He was thorough and smart and made sense. Also, with those dark eyes and sinful voice, it was hard to deny Jack anything. And just the thought that he'd help – used the word "we" just like Cal had – made my heart stutter. He was helping. And in his way, he was trying.

"Fine. But ground rules then are going to be a must."

Jack raised a brow. "You have some in mind?" he asked.

"Please say you want to enforce topless Tuesdays," Cal added.

I rolled my eyes, but Jack seemed to like the idea as much as Cal. "Rule one, I'm not walking around topless," I said quickly. Between Jack's lethal glare and Cal's charm, I needed to rein in my own control before I melted into a puddle of desperate lust.

Cal feigned a pout, and I knew if I didn't hustle through my thoughts, his next suggestion would be naked Wednesdays. But before I could go on, Jack cut me off.

"Fucking," he stated plainly. "I want to hear your rules on that."

A short gasp hit my lungs. He was direct, but this was an issue we had to address. I looked at Cal, he waited quietly, as if wanting to hear the answer to Jack's questions as much as he did.

"The past few days have been confusing," I said.

"No," Jack said curtly. "That's not what I asked. I'm aware of the stress surrounding your life. I'm also aware of the situation Cal and I put you in."

I swallowed hard. Jack was blunt, forcing me to meet his strong words, find my own strength, but there was a hint of raw honesty in his voice. He was taking blame for the situation. Didn't say that I had sex with them both. Didn't put any of it on me. He was acknowledging Cal and his part in this.

"Now's not the time to be vague," he rasped. That hit something deep in my soul. His dark eyes dared me to defy him, but I couldn't.

"You're right," I said with an edge of my own. It was time to get my control back. To harness everything I'd learned from Jack and Cal and apply it. I had always been a good student, time to see the follow through.

Do what I have to do ...

With a deep breath, I looked at Cal, then at Jack.

"I had sex with both of you. Neither instance was planned."

"Do you regret it?" Cal asked. His blue eyes holding a hint of fear, and I couldn't lie. We were past that. All of us were past that.

"No," I said softly. Then, the strangest thing happened. Both their shoulders relaxed just a fraction. Time passed slowly, and there I stood in front of two men I loved ... my heart torn into ragged halves and they each held a piece in their hands.

"Tell me what you want," Cal said. A small smile threatened my lips. He was so good at swooping in and saving the day. While Jack stood still, his jaw ticking and I knew exactly what he was thinking. He wanted to tell me how it was going to be. And part of me wanted to give him that burden and let him.

But I had to find the balance. For myself.

"I love you," I said honestly. Cal smiled and then I looked at Jack, who looked ready to break something. "And I love you." The heat in his dark eyes simmered and a streak of vulnerability crossed his face, as if he wasn't expecting to hear those words from me. "You both hurt me. And I can't commit to anything, or to either of you. I won't."

Cal glanced at the floor and Jack took a step forward. Crossing his arms, he unleashed a wicked grin.

"Is that right?" he asked with enticement in his voice. I was challenging his control. Telling him what I would and wouldn't do and he wanted to play "make Lana heel to my will." And it was a sexy, fun game. One we'd undertaken several times when we were together. That was the past, though. Things weren't the way they'd been when I was first with Jack.

"That's right," I said, lifting my chin with the smallest hint of confidence I felt. Confidence Jack helped me find in the first place. Confidence Cal helped me keep after the fact. Everything was jumbled and mixed, and I couldn't tell which way was up. I could only hope I'd eventually make it to the surface.

"You said you won't *commit* to either of us," Jack repeated my words and tilted his head to the side. "You still have yet to answer my question."

My lips parted briefly, and I didn't know what to say. Cal seemed to catch onto Jack's line of questioning. He examined me like he would his fire truck before taking it out on a call. Intent and thoughtful. A gleam of hope, tied with a sexy smile cracked his handsome face.

"She's not sure she can stay away," he said to Jack. Jack simply nodded, his eyes staying on me the whole time. "She won't commit, won't choose . . . "

"But, she won't give rules on fucking," Jack finished.

"This isn't some twisted challenge I'm putting out there," I defended quickly.

"Uh-huh," Cal said with a wink. "Putting it out there or not, if you say there's a shot with you, Kitten, I'm going to take it."

"There isn't."

Jack tsked. That devilish mouth making me want a lot more than a lecture. "Don't go fibbing now." He took another step, then another, until he was face to face with me. He whispered into my ear, "Your body gives you away." He ran the back of his finger over my nipple. My hard, pouting, nipple that had Cal's mouth on it only an hour ago. The slight feel of his touch grazing the sensitive flesh snapped firecrackers down my spine. "I think there's more than a chance."

Cal cleared his throat from behind Jack and I looked at him over Jack's shoulder.

Jack backed away, grabbed one of the bags by the door that he'd brought, and headed down the hall. Cal followed suit, grabbing a second bag and patting me on the butt and winking at me as he went down the hall next.

I marched down the hallway and saw two bedroom doors, one on each side of the hall. Jack stood in one entry way, Cal in the other.

"Two bedrooms?" I asked.

Cal nodded.

"Where am I supposed to sleep?"

"You tell us, baby," Jack said with a steady tone. "You're the one in charge, right? The one making the rules." He glanced at Cal. "I don't know what the hell went on between you two while I was gone, but she used to like giving up some of that control and letting me have it."

Cal shrugged and leaned against the doorway with all the casualness in the world. "Ah, she's a spirted one. Stubborn. But she likes to take the reins now and again. Sometimes you have to give it to her."

I realized what had happened. The dynamic had shifted. I was up against not just Jack, but Cal too. And I was in trouble.

Because I was finding it hard to breathe just hearing them talk like this. Like they knew me. Because they did. And the worst of it was, they were both right. But getting caught up wasn't smart, and this time at the cabin would already be difficult as it was. Now that Jack and Cal had the upper hand, knew there was a chance, they were fighting dirty. And I couldn't deny sleeping with either of them, or wanting to end everything between us.

I was in big trouble. I could hold to my no commitment policy. I could also hang on to the fact that they hurt me. But sex? The consuming way Jack looked at me and Cal smiled my way? That was going to be the real challenge. Every second reminded me of why we worked so well, in different ways. And nothing about this situation would ever work. Ever.

In fact. It had ended. Gone up in flames the night my house burned down and the truth came out.

"I'm going to bed," Jack said, using one hand to unfasten the top two buttons on his shirt, giving sight to that chiseled chest and what I knew to be rock hard abs even lower. He stared at me while he unbuttoned the third, then the fourth . . .

I shook my head and looked away, only to find Cal faking a

yawn and stretching. Reaching back, he pulled his T-shirt over his head and off, revealing muscles and tattoos and ... damn them both.

"Yeah, I'm going to bed too," Cal said. Keeping his gaze on me. "Are you rethinking topless Tuesdays?"

Before I could answer, Jack peeled his shirt off, showcasing all those perfectly ripped muscles coated in olive skin.

"Based on the way you're staring," Jack said to me. "That'd be my guess."

I forced my gaze away. With a deep breath, I knew I only had one option. I walked past Cal, into his room. I saw him gesture at Jack with a victorious smile. But before either of them moved, I grabbed Cal's bag, carried it across the hall, shoving past Jack, and tossed it on Jack's bed.

Dusting off my hands, I went back into Cal's room and looked at both men, standing in the hallway, staring me down.

"Since you two are both tired, you can sleep together. Sweet dreams." With that, I slammed the door.

Chapter 12

"Okay, thank you anyway," I said and hung up the phone.

Two days had passed and I'd spent every hour calling banks in the Colorado area asking about their lockbox keys. So far, no luck in finding a bank that matched the mystery key my father had left.

"Still nothing?" Cal asked, coming into the living room, bag of mini doughnuts in hand, popping one into his mouth.

I looked at the papers spread out over the couch and me sitting in the middle with no answers. The list was long and I'd only started in the Colorado area. There was a chance it wasn't even in this state, but I hoped it was. Hell, I didn't even know if the bank would still be open.

"No. And all the banks are closed for the holidays now, so I have to wait."

Cal held out the bag of doughnuts, offering me some. I took one and smiled. "Thanks."

He nodded and chewed on another. The way his jaw worked with a light dusting of stubble was hypnotic. A fresh blanket of snow was outside, and no one would ever know it was cold because Cal look so comfortable in well-loved jeans, a white T-shirt, and bare feet.

"We'll find the bank. In the meantime, try to relax."

I scoffed around my mouth of doughnut. Relaxing was something I wasn't good at. Though the setting was perfect for it. The seclusion was nice. Just being away from the city, from anyone like Brock or Anita was *very* freeing. Still, I was holed up with the only two men who had the power to change my world, and had proven they could wreck it within seconds.

"You okay?" Cal asked, as if reading something on my face.

"I just feel a little off."

"It's because you haven't eaten real food today," Jack said, walking in from the kitchen, holding a bowl of salad and roll. It smelled amazing and looked even better. He was a good cook and master salad craftsman. The thing looked more like art than food. He set both in front of me on the coffee table, then stood to look me over as if to assess me.

"What?" I asked.

"I don't like how you look," he replied matter of factly.

I frowned down at my simple jeans and sweater and tried not to cry from the insult. These were the clothes I'd found in the bag Jack brought.

"You're the one that packed this crap and—"

"No, baby, I mean your expression. I don't like how you look so sad." His words were laced with his own kind of sadness, and it made me choke on a deep intake of air. He sat next to me and put the salad in my hands, gesturing me to eat.

I glanced at him, then at the food.

"You really think I'd ever say I don't like the way you *look*?" he enunciated the last word and his fingertip trailed down my

110

throat. He could burn through ice, much less my skin. Every nerve jumped beneath his touch, begging for deeper contact.

I picked up my fork and started stabbing at the salad. I couldn't face him. Not when he was being kind. Not when Cal was being casual. Not like that. I was so close to giving in to the heat and warmth they provided that I needed to get out of this moment.

"Your salad isn't cheering her up," Cal said, taking a purposeful bite of his doughnut. "You want something sweeter, Kitten?"

Cal was so good at keeping things calm and casual.

"Salad is healthy," Jack said.

"Sugar gives you a rush, though," Cal countered immediately.

Refusing to give in to either of them, I put the salad down, grabbed the roll, and took a big bite. Only I couldn't help but moan around the flaky buttery amazingness, which made Jack smile. Something that took my breath away in a whole other fashion.

"Ah, so you're looking for comfort food." I chewed, hoping a full mouth would buy me time. It didn't. Jack just continued on. "I have a question, and I'm going to expect an honest answer. Do you understand?"

I glared at him and hustled through my bite so I could tell him off.

"Hoo-hoo, she's pissed at you," Cal said.

Jack ignored him and continued, flicking the bottom of my chin to have me face him. "I want to know what you want for Christmas."

That was his question? Judging by the lightness in his dark eyes, he'd phrased it that way on purpose to get a rise out of me. I swallowed down the roll and gave my answer honest thought.

111

What did I want?

I looked between Cal and Jack, and wasn't that the question of the century? There was a time when what I wanted was in this room with me. I wanted to let go of fear, gain strength, and prove to myself and to others that I was okay. I wanted to hide in pleasure and never come out. I wanted Jack. Then I wanted to take control, to assert that strength I'd gained and run, sprint far from anything I didn't want to deal with. I wanted to fight. To be chased. I wanted Cal.

I closed my eyes for a moment.

I wanted life to be good. Wanted the man I love. Men I love. I wanted answers. But the past was true to its after effects. I couldn't have any of it. Because I no longer wanted to hide or run . . . I wanted to get lost. And I was alone, while surrounded by the two men on earth that made me feel alive.

What did I want for Christmas?

So many things.

But reality dictated that none of it was possible.

I glanced at the empty corner of the living room. I may not have family left who wanted me. May not have answers or any idea how to get through what was to come, but maybe I could pretend, just for a moment, that life was normal. That one normal thing could bring a piece of simple joy. The kind I hadn't had in a long time.

I looked at Jack and obeyed his command. I was honest. "What I'd like for Christmas is a tree."

He glanced at Cal and nodded. Cal smiled wide. Their secret language in full effect. Jack tucked a lock of hair behind my ear and grinned.

"That, we can do."

*

It was beautiful. The smell of cold air and the sound of two feet on fresh snow crunching beneath my boots was enough to make me think I was on another plane of existence. Not one that was complicated or painful. One that was easy and magical.

We wove through the scattered fir trees. Some smaller than others. Cal walked ahead in his big jacket, an ax slung over his should like some sexy logger. Jack was right behind me. I glanced over my shoulder as we wound through the property. Property, that apparently, was all theirs.

"See anything you like?" Jack asked, with a sexy edge to his voice that had me thinking he wasn't talking about the trees. And he'd be right, since I'd again been caught staring at him.

His thick gray wool coat fit his broad shoulders perfectly and his dark eyes looked bright and wild with the sun reflecting off the snow and lighting him up like an olive-skinned god.

Oh yeah, I saw something I liked . . .

But, feigning disinterest was hard, so I looked ahead once more, only to find Cal's perfect ass in perfect jeans, strutting in front of me like a wall of muscle and manly sexiness. Good Lord, I'd never be able to get away from them.

I turned my attention to the trees and pulled the tie of my coat tighter. Jack had thought of everything and packed us all heavy winter gear that kept us warm and, of course, high-end and fashionable. My chocolate jacket was thick and matched the boots he'd gotten me.

He knew my size in everything. Attention to detail was one of his many qualities. Qualities I wasn't thinking about. At least trying not to think about.

"So, I can pick out any of these trees?" I asked.

Cal turned and stopped, looking around at the scattered forest at our disposal. "Yep, so long as it fits through the doorway, whatever you want."

After taking a moment to examine the nearby prospects, I saw a full beautiful tree with thick needles that smelled amazing. It was barely taller than Jack and Cal, so a six and a half to seven footer, I'd guess.

"I like this one?" I asked.

"Yeah? Well, take your time, we're not in a rush," Cal said.

I looked around . . . nope, this was the tree. "This is it," I said with a smile.

"Okay then, step back," Cal said. I did and Jack was right behind me. With a hand around my waist, he guided us back several more paces.

"You just cut down whatever you want?"

"It's a tradition," he said. I looked at him and something fond flashed across his expression, like he was recalling a pleasant memory. "Bea would drive us out here when we were younger. We'd pick out a tree, cut it down, and bring it home."

My chest stilled for a moment, thinking of Jack and Cal as kids, teenagers even, getting a tree with Bea. Tradition. Something families did. And now they were sharing it with me?

"That's nice," I said softly.

"A few years ago, Cal and I bought the land and put a cabin on it." I turned in his arms and looked at him. "It's a place to escape when life gets . . . " His dark eyes took in every inch of my face, and he looked at me like he could see straight to my soul. "Complicated."

I nodded. Understanding that notion completely. "I can see how things feel less complicated out here." There was nothing but miles of open space, trees, and snow. It was just us. For miles.

A familiar feeling skated through my system like an old drug. One I instantly craved.

Peace.

I'd had this same feeling when I'd felt Jack for the first time. The tremors he calmed with his touch and the fire he ignited all at the same time. The same feeling when Cal took me up on the ladder and let me escape the world for a while then kissed me so softly, I wanted to stay in such a cloud forever.

Complicated.

One thing even all this space couldn't solve was how complicated my life – our lives – had become. Because they were threaded into every fiber of my being. And escape was looking less and less likely. That, in itself, was terrifying because while there may be no escape, there was also nowhere to go from here. It was a choice I couldn't make, even if I wanted to. Which I didn't. That didn't stop the notion from tapping on my temple.

Choose between Jack and Cal . . .

No. I could never.

Just the thought riddled my bones with drama, anger, sadness, and soul crushing pain. There was no good way out of this.

"Tell me how to make that stop," Jack whispered, his lips skimming over my cheekbone. I hadn't realized he'd gotten so close.

"What?" I asked, and looked up into his dark eyes. A snowflake landed on his black lashes, and for a moment, he looked . . . worried.

"Tell me how to make that look stop," he said. I'd seen this expression on his face before. He was upset because he was . . . not in control. Jack had always been able to read me and always encouraged me to say what I needed to say. Own it. So I did.

"I don't know how to make it stop." I was still grappling with the truth that I was doomed. Doomed from ever recovering from

Jack's love and doomed from ever breathing right again from Cal's.

All the hopes I'd once had for Jack and me, then Cal and me, were dashed. All I could hope for now was that now, at this cabin, was a momentary escape.

A flash of white caught my peripheral as it whooshed past me and smacked Jack. I stepped back and saw Jack's left arm covered in snow. Cal was grinning wide and dusting off his snowy hands.

"Maybe you need to lighten up," Cal called, and I didn't know if he was talking to me or Jack or both maybe? "Having fun isn't complicated."

Jack glared so forcefully that the sight alone frightened me. He looked lethal as his intense gaze stayed on Cal and he took a step closer like a cheetah stalking something that it would soon take down.

"Oh . . . it's on now," Jack growled, then quickly scooped two handfuls of snow up, smashed them together forming a ball, and chucked it at Cal, beaning him in the chest.

"Ah, shit," Cal mumbled, shaking off the hit and ducking behind the nearest tree. He wasted no time gathering more ammunition. Jack hustled to a different tree, taking cover, and threw another snowball. If I wasn't mistaken, I thought a smile broke free when the snowball splattered against the tree, millimeters from Cal's face.

"You throw like a pussy," Cal called, then fired his own snowball, barely missing Jack's leg.

"Says the guy who couldn't get it up just now," Jack said, aiming high for Cal's face again.

"Oh, I have no problem getting it up," Cal yelled back, throwing another and hitting Jack's calf as they ducked and ran through trees, hucking snow as they went. "Just ask Lana."

Instead of growling or fussing over his comment, a snowball crashed against my ass. I turned to find Jack smiling and looking guilty.

"What the hell?" I said with a laugh.

"Sorry, baby, you're in between us." He may be talking about the snow war going on, but his words hit hard. Before I could think further on that, another snowball hit my stomach. Cal.

I glared his direction.

"That's it!" I scooped my own snow and threw it fast. First at Cal, then another handful at Jack, as I ran to take my own cover.

"Oh you're in for it now," Jack called from his hideout. A small giggle of delight escaped me as I ducked low and packed another snowball. I wasn't anywhere near as big as the guys, so the tree covered me pretty well. I took the opportunity to make a few snowballs and stock up. Breathing hard, I peeked out and caught a glimpse of Cal and Jack, moving and throwing snowballs as they strategically got closer to me.

"Here, kitty, kitty, kitty," Cal called. Though he may be lighthearted, there was an underlying lust that tainted each word, and my nipples responded instantly and my breathing picked up.

Adrenaline was coursing and this was . . . fun.

With my snowballs in hand, I threw them as I went to gain more ground and a better location, attempting to run and hide at the same time.

Jack caught my movement first and sprung after me. I playfully screamed when his strong arm wrapped around my waist and caught me.

"You're mine now, baby." He turned me to face him and trailed his snowy gloves over my lips and chin, the chill surprising my hot skin. I breathed hard and smiled.

"You'll never catch me," I panted, and spun quickly out of his grip. I made it two feet before meeting a wall of muscle. Cal.

"Caught ya," he smiled, his big arms wrapping me up. I did the only thing I could. I tossed the handful of snow I had at his face. He sputtered and I laughed, getting his grip loose enough to ease out, and I squirmed away. But Jack was right there again, and I was trapped between them.

"Can't get away from me that easy," Jack said against my ear and bit the lobe. His chest was pressed against mine and Cal's chest was against my back, his big hands gripping my hips. For one moment, it felt like a puzzle coming together.

I swallowed hard and look into Jack's eyes, the contact didn't break when Cal's cold nose skimmed over the top of my head.

I turned to see Cal's blue eyes bright and alive. Then he glanced at Jack and shook his head, as if dislodging from the moment. Jack moved back several paces, and Cal's hands fell from me. I felt instantly cold, colder than even the weather should make me feel.

I had been so close to them. Between them. Yet, one thing remained: I wouldn't choose. Despite how the next week went and our eventual goodbye, I would never choose, for good bad or otherwise, between them. Because it was choosing between my heart and soul.

"Let's get you that tree," Cal said, and turned to head back to the one I'd picked out.

Jack was right behind him. He turned and held out his hand. "You coming?"

I did the one thing I shouldn't. I reached for it.

"Yes."

With that, I followed behind the two men that I was desperate for, yet could never have completely again.

Chapter 13

"What can I do?" I asked, walking into the kitchen.

Jack glanced up from cutting a potato. "You can sit there and relax," he said with a gruffness in his voice.

The tree was in the corner, and Cal had gone into town to get some stuff to decorate it with, which left Jack and me alone under the roof.

"No," I said with equal determination. That one got his glance to turn into a glare real quick, so I hustled to finish my statement. "Cal's off doing something, you're making dinner, and I want a job."

"Fucking Cal," Jack muttered and chopped the rest of the potato.

"What does that mean?" I asked, rounding the bar that separated the kitchen from the living room.

"It means he changed you," Jack replied. He turned away to wash his hands. His black sweater looked soft and masculine and was rolled at the sleeves, and paired with dark jeans and a black leather belt made him so mouthwatering I didn't care about dinner. I wanted something else. But his words were too heavy to pull away from.

"Cal changed me, huh?" I challenged. "What? You don't like that I say what I want? That I don't give in to your every command?"

Clenching a small towel, Jack wiped off his hands and stared are me with a sinister and sexy gleam.

"That hasn't changed. You've always voiced what you've wanted. In fact, I recall a time you scratched and clawed and took just that," he said. My mind flashed to the memory he was planting. Jack liked his control, yet he'd gotten me so hot, so needy, I'd demanded and took everything I wanted, and he was right . . . scratched and clawed for more.

"I also remember the follow-up to that encounter," I said.

A small tug of Jack's lips was enough to do me in when he said, "Oh, so do I. And if memory serves, you liked me smacking your ass and commanding you."

I swallowed hard. I did like that. So much. Jack was all strength and dominance, and with every touch and command he gave me the freedom to let go. To put myself in his care. To trust him while reveling in my own strength of letting go.

"I'm different now," I said, a slight tremor in my voice.

"I'm aware." Jack tossed the hand towel on the counter.

"And, you don't like me anymore?" I said with sarcasm.

He scoffed. "You used to drive me nuts. Always straddling the line between innocence and wanton." He took another step. "Begging and demanding all at the same time." His gaze skated over my body. "Now you drive me fucking insane. You're more assertive, but those pretty eyes are looking at me, silently telling me that you still crave being taken over. Which makes this very difficult because I more than like you."

"Stop," I said softly. Because it was too much. I didn't want to hear what he maybe would say next. Especially if it was good.

Because, while I remembered quite a bit, I also remembered one thing vividly. I'd asked Jack once if we were doomed form the beginning . . . and his answer plagued my dreams. *Yes.* Now it was just playing out what we both knew would happen. The end.

"Stop? Are you giving me a number? Because I'm not even touching you."

I closed my eyes for a moment. Our number scale was something Jack had come up with to help ease me out of my fear of men, of sex, of everything.

"Give me a number, Lana," he said, moving closer.

"It's not that simple anymore."

He was so close that I could smell his cologne. His fingers barely dipped into the front of my jeans and ran along the waist.

"Give. Me. A number."

"Six," I said.

"I won't ask you hot or cold, because I feel it. You're hot."

I couldn't deny it, but couldn't give in either. Justifying the single time I'd had sex with Jack since he'd been back was one thing. But going into this was another.

"It's not—"

"That simple?" he cut me off. "I know. But you want to talk about how I left, how I hurt you?"

"You broke me, Jack," I said with anger-laced sadness.

"And I fucking hate myself for that!" he snapped. He cupped my hip. "You're the one in control. Always have been. And you're holding my God damn soul in your fist, Lana. So just this once, stop squeezing."

My eyes shot wide. Jack was nearly shaking from the instinct he was fighting. He struggled when he felt out of control. He was being honest, stripped and raw, and it was hurting him. Despite everything, I loved him. I didn't want to hurt him. Didn't want to make him pay for the past anymore. I wanted to let the pain go. Wanted him to be happy. Wanted to be what he needed. It was an instinct of my own I couldn't fight.

He'd told me once that he didn't share, didn't dance around the truth, and he was going against everything in his nature to stand before me and say what was true. I'd taken control from him. And we both knew I couldn't give it back, because I'd never be able to choose and life would never be the same.

"Say what you need to say," I told him. Just like he'd told me so many times before when I was finding my own strength. "There's no room for vagueness here," I added, and that got his dark eyes to fuel hotter. The hand on my hip squeezed and he looked down at me like a predator.

We both knew I was challenging him, and all I could do was wait to see what kind of dominance he'd reign over me. And I welcomed it.

"You asked me what you could do?" he growled, going back to the original question I'd posed when I first walked in.

I nodded.

His hand slid from my waist, up my breast to my throat, cupping it gently but possessively.

"You can get down on your knees and fuck me with that brassy little mouth of yours." His hot grip on my throat made me instantly wet and a part of my brain kick on that only Jack had the switch to. Submission. The need to obey, the want to do anything he asked – told – was overwhelming.

His whole body shifted, as if recognizing the change in my demeanor.

"Number," he said between gritted teeth.

"Eight, hot. Very, very hot."

Despite his need to control, he still checked my comfort. Always.

"Then you can suck me deep. Show me how much you missed me. Because, baby," he leaned in, his mouth against mine and said, "We both know you did."

Keeping my eyes on his, I gripped his belt and slid to my knees. Instinct took over, as if my body was made to follow Jack. Understood that he was some kind of master over me. And I wanted to be mastered by him.

Kneeling, I looked up at him. "Take off your shirt," I whispered, then added quickly, "Please. I want to see you."

He pulled it off and dropped it to the floor. His chiseled muscles looked so sharp that his abs could cut through his skin. He was all strength and sex and dominance, and he was right, I missed him.

His hand threaded into my hair, gripping a handful at the back of my head. He didn't make me move, didn't say anything, just held me in his tight grasp, and waited. Dominating and demanding, but reading every expression and giving me the slack to take things at my own pace. Like he always had.

I unclasped his belt and opened his jeans. As I tugged them low on his hips, his cock sprang free and my attention was taken. He was long and thick, and exactly what I wanted. But I liked his domination and wanted to feel it. Feel all his strength and get taken over in a way only he could take me.

"You say I drive you insane?" I asked, then licked the head of his cock. His hot skin throbbed against my tongue, so I trailed it along the crown until a low growl escaped him. Looking up I rubbed my cheek against his pulsing shaft and said, "Prove it."

With his grip still firm in my hair, he yanked enough to cause my face to look up at him as he shoved his big cock into my mouth.

I moaned.

He clenched his teeth and pumped his hips.

"You like goading me on purpose?" he asked. "You want to be punished?"

I just moaned again around his cock and sucked the best I could. But his thrusts were intense. He was the one fucking my mouth, and I could tell just how much he'd missed me.

My core shuddered, seeking to be filled. I hated the emptiness. With each push of his hips, he went down my throat and spurred my lust on. I wanted more. So much more I could barely stand it.

I gripped his ass and pulled him closer. Sucking deep and flicking my tongue as I went. His stomach flexed when I tasted the underside of the crown, so I paid special attention to that spot and licked it wildly while continuing to take his thrusts.

"Fuck, baby," he rasped on a strangled breath. Just when I thought he'd come apart, he pulled away and in one quick swoop, had my pants off. "How do you do this to me?" he said, lifting me up and sitting me on the counter.

Ripping my panties away, he spread my legs, and shoved deep inside my core.

"Jack!" I cried his name and held on.

"Say it again," he demanded, and he fucked me hard. My ass slipped along the counter as my shoulders banged into the cabinets behind me. I looked out to see the living room quiet, the one window showing off the night sky. I closed my eyes for a moment at the peace and pleasure of the moment.

A slap sound burst my eyes open and a sting was left high on the side of my ass. My eyes were on Jack and his intense glare.

"I told you to do something," he growled. "Say my name again."

"Jack," I whispered.

"Again," he demanded.

"Jack." The sound of his name tied with the sting of his hand on my skin made my whole body tense with release. I was so close. Wanted to be taken over the edge. I lost myself to him. To his control and need. Because it was my need too. I loved every sting, every ounce of pleasure pain he delivered. He knew exactly what I craved and delivered. Never going too far, never backing down.

He lifted my shirt with one hand while keeping a tight grip around my back, yanking me against him with the other. He sucked my breasts, moving between the two to rain down equal attention. Licking and biting while he plunged deep and hard between my thighs.

He was consuming every inch of me he could get his hands and mouth on and this was the Jack I loved. The Jack that took me over to a different plane of existence. The dark corner I lost myself in, and never wanted to be found.

Heat was rising, my inner walls tightening.

He cupped my face and kissed me, then smiled against my lips. "You're there aren't you?" he breathed and nipped my chin before tonguing his way back between my lips for another drink.

"Y-yes," I moaned as vibrant white pleasure hummed through my veins.

He fucked harder. Faster. His hips slapping against my thighs with each punishing thrust. He never had to ask, he always knew when I was close. But he wanted to hear me say it.

I tensed, my sheath gripping his plunging cock and raining down the beginning of my release.

"Ah, that's it. Come for me, baby."

The sound of the front door shutting caught my attention like a whiplash. My eyes shot open and I saw Cal, standing in the living room, staring at me.

I was in shock, seeing those blue eyes fastened to mine. Jack paused for the briefest moment and turned his head slightly. He didn't look behind him, but he knew Cal was there. His attention was back on me and with the most animalistic expression I'd ever seen on man. He sank deep. I gasped, my eyes shooting wide and my orgasm flooding my body like a live wire.

I shook and trembled and Jack just pounded harder. Fucking me through every intense tremor and wet clench of my pleasure.

Cal didn't take his eyes off mine. Just remained still, and watched me come while Jack continued to take me over.

Jack's shaft thickened and twitched – his hot release flooded me in wave after wave of intensity.

I didn't have time to come down from the high, but Jack kissed me hard. Cupping my face in both his hands as if demonstrating his hold on me in every sense.

I didn't know what to do. I kissed him back, wiggling at the same time until he let me get down from the counter. I pulled my jeans on quickly and Jack tugged up his, not bothering to buckle them.

Cal and Jack exchanged a long, deadly look. Jack just leaned back against the counter I'd just been on and crossed his arms, as if waiting for Cal to say the first word. Cal turned his attention to me and I didn't know what to say. Because the instinct that had gotten me into the position I'd just been with Jack, was the same one screaming at me in confusion.

If I apologized, it was like a betrayal to Jack.

If I didn't, it was like a betrayal to Cal.

My chin trembled as I looked at Cal. Because what I saw in his expression made everything so much worse: empathy.

He wasn't mad. Wasn't enraged, he just looked at me as if . . . he understood. And that broke my heart in a way I couldn't describe. I'd made a choice today. The choice that I wouldn't choose. I'd also let go of the pain from the past. But I'd also gotten caught up in the commanding darkness of Jack. Coming out of that kind of consuming corner was difficult. So I did the one thing Cal taught me how to do, let me do, I ran.

Ran down the hall and into my room, trying not to cry or scream or curse. I just ran until I was out of that moment, out of sight of both of them.

Chapter 14

After a long shower and no hope for clearing my head, I wrapped a towel around myself and walked into the bedroom. Cal had been in the bedroom because there was a T-shirt laid out on the bed. His Golden Fire shirt. The one I'd worn before getting into bed with him weeks ago when we were a happy couple.

My heart lurched at the sight and I ran my fingers over the cotton. God, I missed him. Missed us. How he made life so easy and happy. I missed so many things. But it was his shirt. Not mine.

And it was a statement, one I couldn't make or get lost in at the moment. So I took the shirt and went to put it back in the dresser, when a whiff of Cal's masculine scent caught me. I brought the T-shirt to my face and took a heavy inhale. It smelled like him. The soft material against my face brought tears to my eyes, so I just buried my face in it and tried to get a grip.

The shirt wasn't helping, so I tossed it back on the bed and dug through my bag and pulled on a pair of panties. Panties Jack had picked out when he'd packed. In fact, everything in the bag he'd picked out. And I noticed quickly that the only undergarments he'd given me were white lace thongs.

And there went the Way Back Train again, pulling through my mind attached with all the ghosts of memory past. Like when I'd worn panties just like this and Jack had ripped them away before taking me for the first time. The first man to really make love to me.

I dug through the bag in hopes of finding something that didn't remind me of either of them. But what I found at the very bottom surprised me. My running shoes. The shoes Cal had given me. Jack had packed them for me.

I finally came to a fuzzy set of pajamas.

Thank God he'd packed me warm sleepwear. Pink flannel pants and a long-sleeved shirt. Now wasn't the time for sexy, it was time to be practical. To figure out what I was doing, because being a slave to emotions was not helping anything.

Getting snug in the PJ's and running my fingers through my damp hair, I heard deep voices come from down the hall.

I cracked my bedroom door open slightly and the voices were clear. Jack and Cal.

"There's nothing to discuss," Cal said, his voice echoing down the hall.

"Bullshit, there isn't," Jack said. "You're still trying for Lana."

I put my hand over my mouth. I knew this would be addressed. But had no idea the guys would talk about it without me. Much less not confront me. All I could do was stand and listen quietly.

"Why are you pissed? Because you realize that just because you got to her first, doesn't take me out of the running?"

"It's never been about *first*," Jack snapped the last word.

"Like hell it hasn't," Cal fired back. "I backed off. Because she's important to you. But now, guess what? She's important to me too. Do you have any idea what it was like, what it still is like competing with not just you, but your fucking memory? She loves you, always has, and I have to deal with that every God damn day because I didn't get to her *first!*"

I stifled a gasp, hearing Cal's raw voice deepen on the admission.

"You're right," Jack said, and my eyes shot wide, listening to his strong tone sort out logic. "I couldn't have done what you did. I couldn't handle it. I can barely handle it now, knowing she needs you in a way I can't give her."

A heavy breath was released, and I didn't know if it was Jack or Cal or maybe me? I just clutched the door frame, hoping it would keep me upright, because my knees were shaking.

"You're my family," Jack said. "I'd give you anything. But I can't let her go."

"I know," Cal said with a soft understanding. "I feel the same, brother. I can't let her go either. So, where does that leave us?"

Though I couldn't see them, I knew Jack. Knew the intense gaze he got when thinking through a problem. I could envision him subtly shaking his head.

"I don't know."

That was a direct hit to my lungs. Jack always knew. Always had a plan. Yet I was beyond his logic and coming between them. Bile rose in my throat because it was the last thing I'd ever wanted to do.

"All this will end, eventually," Jack finally said. "We have her now, but I don't know for how long."

I heard a rustle of movement and pictured Cal crossing his arms over his chest. "We won't get another chance after this."

"No, we won't. So, we have now. We have her now. And all we can do is use this time wisely."

"You mean . . . "

"I mean we have to suck it up and let her choose. Give her whatever she needs while we can, and in the end, it's up to her who she takes home with her."

"Fuck," Cal whispered, which was exactly what I was thinking. Because I told them I couldn't choose, and I meant it. But they told me they'd fight. So there we were, all three of us battling each other and the future and our own wills.

"So, that's the plan?" Cal asked. "That we have no plan."

"As much as I hate it, yes. Because she's more important than our plans and we put her in this position to start with."

Another rustle came, and I knew for sure it was Cal this time, pacing and running a hand through his hair like he did when he realized he was lacking control. Both my alpha males were lacking control, and I knew it was killing them. Jack would be standing still. Unimaginably still.

"I hate this feeling," Cal said. "Fear was never my strong point."

Jack scoffed in a way that held a hint of a smile in the note. "I'm aware. It's not my strong point either."

Cal chuckled, but there was nothing funny in his tone. "I thought you told me once that the great Jack Powell wasn't scared of anything."

"I was eleven," he replied quickly. "And you shouldn't talk, seeing as how you live for the rush of danger."

"Not this kind of danger," Cal muttered. "The only time I get worried is when you are." They were brothers, right down to the way they spoke to each other. They depended on one another and looked for different kinds of guidance.

"I'm not worried," Jack said. "I'm afraid."

My brows shot up. I'd never heard the rawness that was tainting Jack's words right then.

"I'm afraid because I know the truth," he finished. "I need Lana . . . but she needs you."

Jack's admission cut through my ribs and pierced my lungs like a sniper shot. I squeezed my eyes shut and sank to my knees.

Gently shutting my door, I rested my head against the wall and two tears slid down my face. One for each of them. They were trying to give me space. Trying to support me and challenge me and love me in the way they knew how, while fighting each other and their own instinct to do it.

I had been crushed, hurting from the "arrangement" they'd made. But everything had shifted.

I was now the one hurting them.

And I couldn't bear it.

The best thing I could do for them was to stay away. A tricky feat, since I had nowhere to go and no money to speak of. But I could try. Tomorrow, I'd figure something out. Right then, all I could do was wipe the tears away and do the best thing for all of us.

Stay away.

"Lana?" A smooth voice beckoned from beyond the brink of sleep. I opened my eyes, at least I tried to. Jack was calling me.

"Lana?" I frowned, hearing my name again. It was Cal this time.

Struggling past a swollen sting, I forced my eyes to creak open. Blur from last night's tears hit me as Cal and Jack came into focus. They were standing over me, looking down.

Last night's events hit me hard.

"I'm sorry," I whispered. It was the only thing that made sense. The sunlight was bleeding through the cracks in the window, showing that it was in fact a new day, bright with consequences and reality.

Jack frowned, Cal just shook his head.

"Nothing to be sorry for. I'm glad you slept in. You needed it."

Jack nodded once in agreement and I wanted to tell them that that wasn't what I was sorry for. I was sorry for what I'd heard – no – sorry for what I was putting them through.

"We need to talk," I whispered as I sat up, hoping to shake the morning – afternoon now – grog off. I didn't know how, but I needed to get away and leave them alone before I caused any more damage. Yes, what I had with each of them was in the past, but that was no reason to make the relationship between the two of them harder.

"I agree," Jack said. Not to my thoughts, but to my previous statement. Yet he spoke so bluntly that it pricked my chest, thinking for a moment he'd read my mind and wanted me gone too.

"I want to check in with the insurance today on the house." Harper and I had a renter's insurance policy. I was waiting on that money so I could get another place to live and rebuild my life. They'd said "after the new year," but staying on top of them would be a good thing. The sooner I got that money, the sooner I had options of supporting myself.

"We can do that, but first we need to talk to you." Cal sat on the bed next to me, while Jack gripped the footboard, slightly bending over, staring my way. They both looked . . . concerned.

"What's wrong?"

"Your phone was ringing off the hook this morning," Jack said plainly. "I ignored it several times, but when the same number kept calling, I answered."

When I frowned, he didn't apologize, just waited for me to challenge him and I knew that look well. He was ready to defend his actions, but Cal spoke up before the exchange of wills passed between us.

"The same number calling back to back had us thinking maybe it was an emergency or . . . "

"Or the asshole after you was being stupid enough to call you and we could finally find him," Jack cut in. Ah, so he was noble in his actions and wasn't invading my privacy just to be frustrating.

"Okay," I acknowledged. "Who was it then?"

"It was the police," Cal said calmly. He tucked a lock of hair behind my ear and I saw Jack glance away. I closed my eyes for a moment to try to handle my crushing chest, but Cal's gaze snared me. "They are officially investigating your father's death as a homicide now. Suicide has been ruled out."

I swallowed hard, but nothing else would flood me. Just that numbness I'd gotten good at the past several weeks.

"You don't seem surprised," Jack said. His grip was tight on the footboard, like he was keeping in all the emotions he couldn't say.

"I guess I'm not surprised. I knew this was a possibility. But, now that it's real, it's . . . " I shook my head. "Hard to wrap my mind around."

Cal nodded and cupped my shoulder, ensuing me with strength as if he knew I needed it. "They want to ask you some questions if you're up for it." He set my cell next to me. "We can either go to the station or they'll come here."

"They aren't coming here," Jack cut in, his eyes narrowing on Cal when he went to argue. "No one knows of this place or that she's here, and I want to keep it that way. Whoever set fire to the house is still out there."

Cal exhaled loudly and shot Jack a glance before saying to me, "He's got a point. So, if you'd like, Jack and I will take you to Denver today to talk to the police."

"But, we're staying with you at all times and you're coming right back here," Jack added.

I tried to glare at him, but couldn't. It was the most incredible thing I'd ever seen. Being surrounded by both Jack and Cal was incredible. They both came from a place of concern. I knew that. But how they went about it was so different it was almost humorous.

I smiled slightly and adjusted in bed, tucking my feet beneath me. Because despite their caring or my safety, I needed to stick to my plan of leaving.

"I would appreciate a ride into Denver, but then I won't be coming back," I said.

Jack laughed. Honest to God laughed, and it caught me off-guard both with confusion, surprise, and glee because the laugh was hypnotic.

"You are kidding yourself if you think that's going happen." His dark eyes zeroed in on me. "But leave it to you to fight against every damn thing I say."

"I'm not trying to fight you."

"Good," he said. "Because I'm not going to go through this with you again, Lana. You are in danger. You're staying here until all this shit is straightened out. Do you understand?"

A low simmering growl broke my throat. I used to love when he said that to me. Demanded. Put me in his care, his command, and I trusted him. I still did, despite my best efforts, but I wasn't going to stay and watch a life-long friendship implode because of me.

"I should be getting money from the insurance claim, and I'll—"

"You'll what? Stay at a different hotel? Find a new place? What about the person who set your house on fire? The person who hit

135

you and Bea with their car? You think they'll just magically leave you alone?"

Jack's words were sharp and cutting. Judging by the look in his eyes, that's what he was going for. Because I was scared that this would never end. And the person who obviously wanted me dead was still out there. Worse, I was certain is was Brock.

"I can't stay here," I tried to sound direct, but felt anything but.

"Yes, you can. And I'm with Jack on this. I won't let you go either."

"I'm ruining you!" I snapped and looked at Cal. He frowned.

"What do you mean?" Jack asked pointedly.

Truth time. There was no other choice than honesty.

"I heard you last night," I said. "I'm not going to choose, and I'm not going to come between you. I'm sorry for how this past week has gone. I'm sorry for a lot of things, but I'm not going to stay here and create more animosity between you two. I won't. I lov—"

Both of them perked up and their eyes fused to mine. I just shook my head and looked down.

"Don't stop talking now," Cal said.

"Say what you need to, Lana," Jack agreed. "Otherwise, I'll interpret your half-explanations and I can guarantee it's better in my mind."

With a heavy breath, it took everything not to take the bait. Because I was ready to scream, "I love you, jackass!" but couldn't. It'd make everything worse.

"I'm tired of being scared. I'm tired of running," I glanced at Cal, then met Jack's eyes, "and hiding."

It was painful to say and even more painful to see their expressions fall. The truth was, I wanted to be lost. Wanted to not be in this situation anymore. I didn't want to be a bad thing in either of Jack or Cal's life.

"Running or hiding aside, you're going to stay here until your safety is no longer an issue," Jack said. "The idea that you're causing problems between Cal and me is irrelevant and not completely true. If you heard us last night, then you also heard that *you* are our concern." He waited a beat until I was fully staring at him. "Do you understand?" he asked once more with less venom. And that was what did me in. Jack was *asking*.

"Yes," I whispered.

"Don't worry about me, I'm fine," Cal chimed in. "Jack?"

"Perfectly fine," Jack said confidently. "And I'm not looking to trap you. I just want to keep you is all."

"See?" Cal winked. "Let's get through the New Year, figure out what this key is that your dad left, and sort all these questions out about the fire and his death, then we can move on from there."

"Move on?" I asked, looking at Cal.

He nodded. "I have every intention of moving on from this whole mess I – we – made with you. And I'm sure as hell going to try to get you to move with me."

"In the meantime," Jack said, cutting in. "Do you want to go to the police station?"

"Yes." I wanted to hear what they'd found about my dad. Wanted to be a part or help in any way I could.

"And, after, you're coming back here," Cal said, half asking, half clarifying. I looked at him and had to trust that he and Jack really were okay. That things would somehow work out. They knew my stance. I knew theirs. Now it was time to let life play out how it would.

Do what I have to do to get through this . . .

"Yes," I said.

With a smile, Cal nodded, and I was pretty sure Jack grinned as well. I was treading in dark waters and I couldn't pull myself to shore. The only alternatives were to keep fighting the current, or drown in the sea.

They left me to get ready, and as I watched two strong, intense men walk away, knowing they wore their pride on their sleeves, I couldn't help but wonder if drowning in that kind of darkness would be so bad.

Chapter 15

I didn't realize how bitter the air was until I was sitting in the Denver police station. After having several days of breathing in the crisp scent of wide open space back at the cabin, the smell of the city was lacking. Or maybe it was the situation I found myself in.

I sat near Detective Darrell Selander's desk and shifted a bit in the plastic seat. It squeaked and jiggled a bit on its uneven legs. The detective ran a palm along the side of his stiffly gelled salt and pepper hair. His face held signs of wear that came with twenty-plus years on the force. He looked like an older, rougher version of Elvis.

The faintest scent of Cal's spicy soap danced beneath my nose. It was the only thing of comfort I clung to at the moment. That, and the way Jack's eyes constantly swept over me from across the room, as he spoke with another officer.

Cal's hand rested on my shoulder, letting me know he was there, right behind me, supporting me.

"Can you walk me through what you did the night of your father's death one more time, Miss Case?" Darrell asked, clicking his pen and hovering it over an open file of what looked to be my original statement.

"I was watching my house burn," I said.

He nodded. "I know you've had some issues of your own . . . "

"Issues of her own?" Cal said, that fierce alpha voice coming to the surface. "Brock VanBuren assaulted her, her house was set on fire, and weeks before that, her home was burglarized and her car vandalized. These aren't issues, this is a big fucking problem."

"Yes, you're right," the detective said with a slight catch in his voice. Couldn't blame him. Cal was large and intimidating as hell when he was angry. "I just want to go over everything, make sure nothing was missed, because we're taking this case very seriously. We think the trouble you've had, Miss Case, is related to your father's murder."

"No shit," Cal muttered.

Detective Selander clearly chose to ignore his comment and move on.

"If there is a connection to be made to Brock VanBuren, we want to make sure we present the strongest evidence possible." He flipped through several papers on his desk, looked them over, frowning, then looked back at me. "You're still waiting for the assault charges you brought against him to be seen by a judge?"

"That's right," I said.

The detective nodded. "But Brock was in the county jail the night the fire hit. We can account for his whereabouts during that time, but before and after is where it gets fuzzy, which is why we need to have something ironclad."

I nodded. It was starting to sound like the detective was really trying to solve my father's murder and was thinking Brock wasn't innocent in all this.

"But you said that your home and car were broken into before the fire," he flipped through more papers. "You reported nothing was stolen, though? Did you know it was Brock VanBuren that broke in? Did you see him?"

My lips pressed tight, because no, I hadn't. I'd found out after that it was Brock because Erica told me. She had been there, driving the car that he took off in. I didn't want to incriminate her, accidentally or not. It wasn't worth the risk of her getting into trouble because Brock used her. She wouldn't hurt me.

"It wasn't until Brock showed up at my house and assaulted me that I knew for sure he was behind everything. But now that my house is gone, discussing how it was broken into prior to the fire doesn't really matter."

"It establishes a string of behavior if you saw him in your house."

But I didn't see him. Yet I couldn't say that without the likely follow-up question, asking how I did know then.

"I reported what I knew at the time of the robbery. Can we discuss my father now please? You said this was now a homicide."

He nodded. "We are trying to make a timeline to narrow down suspects, though typically these kinds of cases don't stray far from home or motive."

"Alright. Then, how can I help?"

"I want to make sure the timeline of your whereabouts is clear." My lips parted, and the last statement from the detective ticked through my mind. Was I a suspect? "Your father was killed the afternoon of the same night your house burned. Before you got to your home the night of the fire, where were you?"

"Before or after she was assaulted?" Cal asked with raw anger. He was catching on to the same thing I was. I was being questioned in a way I hadn't been ready for.

"Let's start with before," the detective said. "What were you doing?"

141

I searched my memory for that day, but it was all a blur of stress. "I think I ran some errands."

"Were you with anyone?"

"No, not until I got home and Brock showed up."

"Showed up, pushed his way in, and assaulted you?" he clarified.

"Yes."

"Then you went to the hospital."

"Yes."

"And, after that?" His questions were coming fast and I did my best to keep up.

"I went to bed," I said honestly.

"Not your own bed, obviously."

"No," I said and glanced over my shoulder at Cal. "I was at Cal's house."

"And you left on foot?"

"Yes."

"Why?"

"We had an argument."

The detective glanced at Cal, his frantic pace of questioning slowed. He scooted a little closer and leaned toward me. "Perhaps we should talk alone?"

Another dose of realization hit. The way he was glancing at Cal, then at me, made the detective's thoughts play out clearly on his expression. He thought Cal was an issue.

"I want Cal here," I said confidently.

The detective still wasn't certain, and glanced at Jack, who was now walking our way.

"You seem to have an entourage everywhere you go, Miss Case."

"That's because no one around here is going to protect her," Jack interrupted, coming to stand on the other side of me. Being flanked by both men, feeling their strength, was powerful. Made me feel powerful. And safe.

"We are doing everything we can," the detective assured us. Yet his assurance did little to comfort me.

"Are you? Then why are you wasting our time questioning a victim of this situation instead of starting with people who clearly have motive and have taken action in hurting Lana? Like Brock VanBuren."

Jack's tone was cut and dry, and made the detective do his own seat shifting now.

"He was in jail the night of the fire."

"That doesn't mean he's alone in his actions. He was caught at her house. Lana is the target, yet she sits here, answering your questions while no progress is made."

The detective pinched the bridge of his nose and sat back in his seat. There was honest frustration in his movements. Like, he was actually trying and getting stonewalled himself.

"We are looking into financials, the Case-VanBuren business, and the estate as whole. These things take time, but there are motives where there's money, we just haven't found anything yet that justifies why Carter Case was murdered."

There was a lot of money and a name like VanBuren at stake. Things couldn't be going easy. "But Anita stood to gain everything, didn't she?" I asked. I only knew the one detail Anita had said at my father's funeral. That I wasn't in the will. So, everything must have gone to her.

"Yes, she gains to a point. But she didn't need Carter dead to have access to the company or money. Everything appears to be jointly connected."

"Have you spoken with Anita? Does she know about my father not having committed suicide after all?"

"Yes, we spoke with her attorney. We will question her again as well. We're just following up with everyone, since the classification of his death changes things."

I glanced at my hands. So many questions swirled. Part of me was happy my father hadn't committed suicide. Part of me was even angrier that someone took his life away. There was no upside in a situation like this, because the outcome remained: my father was gone.

And I'd loved him. Despite everything, I loved him and my stomach dropped whenever I thought about the fact that I'd never see him again.

"How did you figure out he was killed instead of ..." I couldn't finish the question. Jack's hand was now on my other shoulder. Both of them behind me. Right there to fight with me.

"There was no gun residue on your father's hands," the detective said with empathy. "Which means he wasn't the one who held the gun to his head."

I flinched, thinking of that detail, and cold shivers broke over my skin.

"That's why we're re-examining the case from start to finish."

"I appreciate that," I said, and looked up to find the detective's eyes had softened a little.

"If you think of anything else, you can call me anytime," he said and glanced at Cal, then Jack. Everything in that glance felt wrong. Like he was piecing together the fact that I was one woman, with two men behind me. It must look odd, but everything about Cal and Jack felt right.

No matter how it seemed – bad or otherwise – being with both of them made me feel better and stronger than being without them. They felt right. The exact opposite of how I'd spent my life up until I'd met them.

"Thank you, Detective."

I rose from the seat, encased on each side by a wall of muscles and yummy smelling man. Cal with his casual jeans and T-shirt and Jack in a suit, it was the dark and light I needed to get through this. And no matter how it looked, in that moment, I was grateful for both of them.

Chapter 16

It was dark when we got back to the cabin and every bone in my body felt frail and chilled.

"You okay?" Jack asked, shutting the door behind us. I just hugged my arms close to my body.

"Yeah. I just feel . . . " I closed my eyes for a moment. "Cold."

Jack's gaze went dark. He didn't like the word cold. He'd told me once that when it came to me, he couldn't work with "cold." Which was why he kept me hot.

Right then, I wanted to lean in and steal some of the heat radiating off of him. But I couldn't. I also couldn't go to the warmth strewing off of Cal. I was stuck, feeling cold, in more ways than one.

"Why don't you go get into your pajamas?" Jack said.

I nodded and did just that. Pulling on the soft material of my pink PJs was instantly comforting. When I walked back to the living room, Cal was kneeling over the fireplace, poking at the roaring flames, and Jack had just set three mugs of steamy cocoa down on the coffee table.

A smile split my lips because it was clear that Jack took my internal and external heat very seriously.

"Come here," Cal said, and patted the plush area rug beside him, which was positioned right in front of the warm fire. I sat down and Jack handed me a mug, then one to Cal. He came to sit on the other side across from me.

I took a sip of my cocoa and—

"Whoa, this is good. What's in it?"

"Whipped cream vodka," Jack said, and took a drink himself.

"I make mine with love, but whatever," Cal said in a teasing voice and took a sip himself.

Smiling over the rim of my cup, I took another long swallow and glanced between Jack and Cal. I licked my lips, tasting the sweet chocolate, as I found myself staring down Jack's perfect mouth. The day's shadow was on his face and the way the fire lit up his dark eyes was so sexy and sinister, he could be the devil asking for my soul and I'd happily turn it over.

Wait, I'd already done that.

Trying to gain composure, I glanced the other direction to find Cal, his T-shirt clinging to his broad chest and those blue eyes wild with light. He was almost angelic-looking with the halo of orange glow behind him.

"If you keep biting your lip like that, I'll start to get the wrong idea," Cal said.

I blinked hard, looked at my cocoa, and took another swallow when I heard Jack's smile. It was so silent and so engulfing that it could be heard.

I hesitantly met his gaze.

"She's *nervous*," Jack said with victory in his tone.

"Why are you saying that like it's a good thing?" Cal asked.

Jack's eyes just stayed on me. "Because it is."

I knew very well what being *nervous* around Jack meant. And he knew it too. The first night I'd met him we'd established

147

quickly that when my nerves got the better of me, it was my body responding to Jack. Responding to his heat.

"You still cold?" Jack asked, with a tilt of his head and challenging tone. "Or are you hot?"

"I'm fine," I whispered.

Jack tsked. "You're more than fine. I can see it on your face. Admit it."

"Why?" I snapped back.

"Because I want to hear the truth from you."

Jack was the one who encouraged me to always say what I wanted – needed – to say. So long as it was the truth, it was worth saying. But nothing felt that simple. Still, I couldn't back down from his challenge.

"I'll give you the truth, but I can't promise you'll like it."

"I would expect nothing less," Jack said. "Now say it. Hot or cold?"

With a deep breath, I admitted, "Hot."

Cal realized that this went deeper than the fire and he caught on real quick. Because I saw the thing he made me believe in: hope.

"So long as you're answering questions and offering up the truth . . ." Cal scooted closer.

"Wait," I glanced between Jack and Cal. I had to get some kind of control of this moment, otherwise, I'd lose myself to it and them before I could pull back. And I promised all of us that I wouldn't be an obstacle. "When did this turn into ganging up on Lana?" I asked.

Cal smiled. "That's been going on since day one, Kitten."

I huffed and worked another angle. "I think we need more rules."

"Like?" Jack asked, intrigued.

"Like, no touching," I said and his gaze went black with annoyance, and Cal just looked bummed out.

"I can't touch you, huh?" Cal asked.

"Neither of you can." I took another sip, hoping the vodka would bring a bit more liquid courage with it. Because when the two men exchanged a knowing glance, I knew that they were speaking in their silent way again.

"Okay, back to the truth then," Jack said. "Neither of us can touch you, but I want to hear about what you like touching."

I frowned. "What?"

"You heard me," he said.

"Yeah, but I don't know what the point is."

"The point is, you offered up terms of honesty in exchange for no touching. Those terms were accepted."

"Time to pay up," Cal said, and took his own drink of cocoa.

Great. Somehow they'd managed to sneakily turn this turn into truth or dare, minus the dare and upping the truth while I sat over the flames while two men closed in on me. Not physically, but in every other way possible. Painted into a corner wasn't the half of it.

"Do you miss being touched?" Jack repeated his question, only more direct this time. Damn him.

"Yes."

"Care to elaborate?"

"No."

There, he was getting his truth and I was trying to hold myself together. He obviously didn't like my tactics, but he chose to start this little battle of wills. I was staying true to my terms.

"Alright, then it's up to me to interpret." He scooted closer until his mouth hovered over my ear. "I also like pulling from memory to support such interpretations." His closeness put the fire to shame and he whispered so only I could hear. "I recall that every time I touched your pussy, you were already wet and hot. Which means you obviously liked some kind of touching before that."

I kept still, because if I turned to look him in the eyes, my mouth would meet his. Jack was baiting me again. Whispering every naughty thing to make my blood pressure spike. Though Cal couldn't hear, a tremor of wicked lust beat beneath my skin, knowing he was in the room while Jack continued his verbal seduction.

"Would you like to know one of my favorite memories in particular?" Jack asked quietly.

I nodded subtly.

"It was when I sank my fingers inside your tight heat and you rode them just as hard as when I followed with my cock."

I didn't gasp, I couldn't, because air refused to come to me. My heart sped up, my mind pulling up every vivid moment of that night I was with Jack. How he felt. His touch.

He sat back, clutching his mug in a single hand and resting his elbow on his bent knee. He was sinful when he was dominantly cocky.

"Well, now that you're done dishing secrets like a schoolgirl," Cal said, "I need a warmer. Would you be so kind?" He held out his mug to Jack, who eyed it like a rodent. Clearly he didn't want to go anywhere, but he grabbed Cal's cup and headed into the kitchen.

Cal's blue eyes landed on me and there was something dangerous and consuming in them. I knew that look. I'd been on the receiving end of it several times before and it usually happened right before he made me come.

"I'm not entirely deaf," he said. He leaned in, face so close to mine I could lick my own lips and taste his in the process. "I heard your hips mentioned?"

His tone was deadly, and I didn't know if I should say anything or not. But, the truth was, yes, Jack had mentioned something along those lines.

"If you're taking a trip down memory lane, then I'd like to toss one out for your consideration." He glanced at my mouth and grinned when he saw me bite my lip. "I think of your sexy little hips frequently. Especially the way you rock them while riding my tongue."

My entire chest filled with lust so thick it was like concrete had been poured in my lungs. It was easy to remember how Cal had made me crazed with passion, then pulled me up to straddle his face, and just thinking of that masterful tongue of his had me tucking my legs beneath me and trying not to squirm at the recollection.

"Do you have any idea how sweet and ripe you taste?" Cal kept going. "Every part of you is delectable. Those pretty nipples of yours are particularly addicting."

Jack walked back into the room and I struggled to exhale.

He handed Cal his cup, then took his seat again. I used the space to regain my composure.

"I think you both have interpreted enough," I said, then took a long swig of cocoa.

"You sure?" Jack asked with mock concern. "Because I was just trying to be thorough, since you don't want to answer the questions thoroughly yourself."

"For the sake of this thoroughness, I can keep going too," Cal said, and tossed a casual wink at me.

"Next question," I said, as sternly as I could. The slight buzz of the vodka helping and also making my body pulse in a way that was difficult to manage. Or it was Cal and Jack's wicked words and deep stares.

"Sticking on this touching topic," Cal started. "Do you miss touching me?"

That, I wasn't ready for. Part of me wanted to be honest. Wanted to think for a moment that somehow this would help me purge them from my system. Talking through everything would somehow make this idea of moving away from them easier.

Or it could be a heavy dose of denial. Because I wasn't moving. I was sitting. Stunned and wet and overheated. And, damn them both, I wanted to reach out. For them. For those memories they just threw between us. They were so vivid and heavy that I thought reaching out and grabbing them was actually possible. Holding on to those would be the only thing I could hold on to once this was all over . . .

I hated the thought, but that was reality. It was best. And it would happen. So, for now, I was on the stand, answering their questions.

"Yes," I said and looked at Cal. "I miss touching you." I glanced at my hands in my lap before meeting Jack's face. "And I miss touching you."

"Explain," Jack said quickly and firmly.

I parted my lips to say no, but when he lifted his chin, like he was expecting – maybe even hoping – for just that, I thought twice. If I didn't give some details, each of them would fill in the blanks for me. And only add to the growing need I had for both of them. It was time to take some power back. Find my strength and control in a way I'd learned from the two men before me.

"There are lots of things I miss," I said with the silkiest voice I could muster and crawled toward Cal. I felt Jack's eyes on my every move, so I went slowly. "Like right here." I reached out and trailed my fingertip along Cal's tattooed bicep. His muscle strained and jumped against my touch. "You flexed whenever I ran my tongue along your ink," I said, looking up into those endless pools of blue.

I gently kissed his bulging muscle and his whole body shot hard with tension. He was trying not to touch me back. Serves him right for the crap he pulled, recounting intimate moments and getting me hot and bothered. "But, my favorite thing . . ." I whispered, lips never leaving his arm, "was when I . . ." I bit the hard muscle, and he hissed.

I backed away and smiled.

Cal growled and looked ready to jump on me and rip the clothes from my body.

"Sheathing the claws but bringing out the teeth," he said with a hungry expression. He liked it when my rougher side came out, and yes, I missed it. Missed him. Missed the way his entire body reacted to me. Like it was doing now. And my whole being was begging to keep going. To reach out and taste – bite – some more.

But when I saw Jack's hot glare out of the corner of my eye, I turned to face him and scooted just an inch closer.

"And you," I said with a hint of reprimand. "You challenge me, yet forget what I hold over you." I slowly reached beneath his button up, my fingers skimming along his hard torso and it took all my will to keep from pushing him down and tearing his shirt off.

"You hold much over me," he whispered, and I couldn't let the raw softness of his voice melt me. Couldn't give in.

"I miss touching you like this." Slowly my hand trailed from his chest, down his stomach. "The way your muscles tightened every time your hips moved was my undoing . . . " My mouth hovered close to his, just as my hand reached his side. "But, what I miss most . . . is this—"

I pinched his side and Jack jolted, and a small, quick laugh broke the sound barrier.

I backed away and he just growled at me, looking beyond pissed off. Cal, however, looked shocked and elated.

"Holy shit, you're fucking ticklish?" Cal said to Jack.

"No," Jack snapped.

"Even I didn't know that!" Cal chuckled and winked at me. "Nice work."

"I'm not fucking ticklish," Jack said.

My eyes shot wide and a huge smile couldn't help but split my face, because he was hiding his own amusement.

"Aw, don't be sad," Cal said. "The tickle monster isn't real. You'll be okay."

Jack muttered a curse and just shook his head. "He'll never shut up about this now, you know that, right?" he said to me.

I shrugged and laughed. "I was just being honest. Like you asked."

"So, you get to touch us, but we can't touch you?" Jack asked.

"Yep. Unless you'd like to amend those rules, then I don't have to touch you either."

Both of them answered in unison, "No."

It shouldn't make me as happy as it did, but . . . it did. I wasn't looking to hang control over their heads, just trying to survive this time with them without destroying their friendship or what was left of any kind of soul I had. Because I wanted them so much it was starting to physically hurt. And they wanted me back. So, the struggle lay within myself to stick to this arrangement.

"I warned you," I said.

Jack leaned in and in a deadly sexy tone, whispered, "But, you made the rules. You'll pay for that little stunt, baby. I promise you that."

And that made a whole new memory flash to mind, when thinking of that last time Jack punished me. His hand slapping my ass was one of the best experiences of my life. And I so badly wanted to take him up on his threat.

No, no touching.

Jack finished off his cocoa, then looked at Cal. "She's got some spark."

"Yeah, she does," Cal said.

Between the naughty thoughts, sexy smiles, and even sexier glares, I was having a hard time seeing, thinking, or even feeling straight.

"It's past midnight," Cal said, glancing at his watch. Jack nodded and got up and walked down the hall.

Did I miss something? I looked at Cal, who had a big grin on his face. Those dimples making crazy things happen to my heart. Jack came back into the room with two gifts and set them in front of me.

"It's officially Christmas," Jack said, and resumed his seat on the other side of me. I looked at the two packages in front of me. One was wrapped in white paper with silver flecks on it, the other was in red glossy paper.

"You didn't need to do this," I said, looking between the two of them. I wished I had gotten them something, but everything had been crazy. Yet, somehow, they managed this for me.

"Don't go getting all sad until you open them," Cal said, reaching out to touch my shoulder, only to drop his hand before he did. Respecting the no touching rule. Only I felt awful for drafting such a rule, especially when I wanted his touch.

"Open it," Jack coaxed.

With a deep breath, I took the red one. "That's from me," Cal said and bounced a little. Which was adorable, since he was large, tattooed, and everything about him could be intimidating if he wasn't so wonderfully caring.

I ripped at the paper and opened the box. I pulled out a blue Golden Fire T-shirt. Only it wasn't Cal's, it wasn't oversized. It was my size.

"The guys said you're one of us and you needed your own shirt," he said with a shrug. But, when I looked and saw a small piece of paper on the bottom of the box, I reached in and realized it was a recipe card.

"Bea's cranberry sauce?" I asked.

Cal nodded. "She refuses to pass it down to anyone. It's just for family. She gave it to me after I met you."

Tears stung my eyes. This was too much. It was simple, yet said something more than I could dare to hope. Something I'd once hoped for. Family. A sense of belonging. And Cal was the man who was so good at giving me that.

"Thank you," I whispered. I stopped myself from hugging and kissing him, which was one of the hardest things I'd ever done.

He nodded. "You're welcome."

I looked at Jack, his was the white present. I opened the box and unrolled something in tissue paper. I pulled out a small tree branch. No, wait, it wasn't a tree branch. But it looked like it. It was a creamy color and felt fragile and rough to the touch. But the intricate pattern it was in made me think it was some kind of decorative piece.

"Thank you," I said, smiling.

Jack just grinned. "You don't know what it is, do you?"

"Of course I do," I said, and looked the branch thing in my hand again.

"Truth," he reminded me.

I pursed my lips and said, "No, I'm sorry. I'm not sure what it is."

"Good. That means that you've never seen it before."

I looked at the piece again. Nope, couldn't say that I have.

"It's lightning," Jack said in a calm tone.

My eyes shot wide and I looked at him, then at the mystery item in my hand. He had told me once that I was his light within the storm. Everything from that moment had changed because I knew then that we were unique. Our relationship was unique. And he'd made me feel special. Like he needed me.

"How . . . how is that possible?" I whispered. Leave it to Jack to find a way to give me lightning.

"It's sand that was hit by lightning. Forever frozen from the place it marked."

The tears I'd been fighting back lined my eyes. I couldn't fight the need to reach out. To either of them. So, I did just that.

I wrapped my arm around the back of Jack's neck and pulled him in for a kiss.

When his lips met mine, I kissed him hard and deep and swiftly, backing away before I could start, because I'd get lost.

I turned to Cal and pulled him in by the T-shirt and he crashed his lips on mine. Stealing one hot, brief kiss.

"Thank you," I whispered against him. Then pulled back to look at Jack. "Thank you both so much."

Getting pegged between a hot black stare and smoldering blue gaze, I didn't know what to do. I knew what I wanted to do.

What I wanted to say. But I couldn't. I loved them. And it was tearing apart everything.

I gathered my treasures and stood.

"This was more than I ever expected," I said. And I meant that beyond the gifts. Jack and Cal were beyond anything I ever thought my life would obtain. And I would lose them.

With a final look at them, I walked to my room and shut the door. A loud exhale left my chest, because it took everything I had not to throw open the door and go running, begging for them to love me.

But, which one?

That was the question of my life. And, instead of answering it, I clutched my gifts and tried not to cry.

Chapter 17

I sank back into the large claw-foot tub. It had been a hell of twenty-four hours, but with Christmas officially over, I didn't know how to feel other than exhausted.

All I could think about were Jack and Cal. Their gifts were beyond thoughtful and spoke to the kind of love we have.

Had.

The word stuck to my skull like hot glue and I hated it.

Deep breath.

The water sloshed and I looked around the nice bathroom. The stone shower cave thing was in the corner and the bathtub had its own nook in the opposite corner. The steam wafted around me as I tried to think through everything. But my brain just flipped me the giant middle finger, because all I thought about was the taste of Cal's skin and the feel of Jack's hands.

I reclined further and closed my eyes . . .

"Enjoying yourself?" Jack asked, and I jumped with alarm. He was sitting on the edge of the tub, his hair slightly ruffled, like he'd be running his hands through it, and his white button-up shirt was rolled at the sleeves.

"I was until you scared me to death."

His eyes jumped from my face to my breasts, which were bobbing at the top of the water. Not that the clear water concealed much anyway. I tried to slink a little lower in the tub.

"That won't help you. I can see everything. And your rules said nothing about looking."

"Is there something you want?"

"Yes," he said instantly, and I cursed myself. I had to stop asking that, because the way he looked at me made me want to beg him to take it. And I would give him whatever he wanted.

His hot stare roamed over me again, and it was useless trying to hide from him. Especially because I wanted him to jump into the water with me.

"I remember the last time I was in the bath with you," he said softly. His eyes closed for a moment like he was in pain. "Feeling you for the first time."

"Jack," I whispered his name, in a plea to stop, to continue, I didn't know. But the memory burned my mind and yes . . . it was painful. In a way only beautiful memories could be.

"That was the night you told me you loved me." For a brief second, a thick blanket of hope passed between us. He glanced away and flexed his hand once before returning with a steel expression. "But I didn't come to reminisce." His words snapped me back to reality. Only Jack could play indifferences like it was little more than flicking a light switch. "I need to speak with you about something important, something that will make you happy."

"Okay," I said with weariness.

"But first, I want something."

"Of course you do."

"Lift your no touching rule."

"Can't," I said quickly, because if I hesitated too long, I'd say okay. Then I'd likely do a repeat of the last time I was in the bath with him and there'd be no turning back.

"A compromise then. Let me touch you from the knee down."

I frowned. The knee down? Surely there was nothing sexual about that.

"Alright," I agreed, and just as I got the word out, he sank his hand in the water, gripped my ankle and drug it up to rest on his thigh. I adjusted my shoulders, still reclining in the tub, just as he pressed his thumbs into the arch of my foot.

I moaned and relaxed completely.

"See, baby? Letting me touch you isn't so bad," he purred like a big cat before consuming its prey. He was rubbing my foot, relaxing me to a point of total bliss. The kill shot must be coming. Because Jack never played fair.

"You wanted to talk to me," I pushed, trying to keep my wits. When he pressed his fingers into my instep, I arched, my breasts coming out of the water. I couldn't help it, though, it felt amazing. Besides, my leg was on his and he could see a lot more with my legs spread than my breasts.

"My guy found the bank that key belongs to."

"What?" I said. "Really!"

He nodded, a happy expression lacing his face.

"Wait, you have a guy?"

"Yes." He rubbed my foot some more and I was back to a puddle. "The bank is in Highlands Ranch. It's older and not in high demand, but it will be open the day after New Year's."

"That's perfect. We can go first thing in the morning before Anita meets with the company sellers." Because whatever, if anything, was in that lockbox, it would be wise to know about it before she touched my father's company.

He nodded.

The finish line is in sight. Whatever was going on, it was all tied together. That I believed, and so did Jack and Cal. Soon. This would all be over soon.

"Thank you," I said with everything in me, because I was truly grateful. For so much.

He just glanced away and rubbed my foot. When his eyes hit me again, I saw the determined face of lust. He was so good at changing gears, the simplest touch or look could set my blood on fire. I knew by the expression on his face that warm and fuzzy time was over.

"I'll ask you one more time to lift your no touching rule," he said. Dominance dripped from his voice, and I knew the instinct he was trying to fight. His hands gripped my foot in a way that made me think he was putting in effort to not touch me further. I knew Jack. Knew his palms were itching for more than one thing. And my skin was begging to have it.

But I had to stay strong. Think of Jack. Think of Cal. Think of their friendship. Messing up anything between them was not my goal. I would have to leave at some point, and while New Year's was right around the corner, I just had to make it with the slivers of my heart intact until then.

I shook my head, because I couldn't tell him no out loud. Something he picked up on, because that dark look went even darker.

"Fine. If you won't allow me further access to you, then you'll touch yourself," he said with all the authority in the world.

He looked between my legs and I went to move, but he held my foot tight, forcing me to stay right where I was.

"If you can tell me honestly that you don't want to come for me, I'll let you go and leave you to bathe alone."

He waited. If he was sticking to my rules of no touching, I had to stick to his of being honest. I couldn't deny it. I wanted to come. So much my body ached from the need.

When silence passed between us, Jack took in my whole body once more, then said, "Take your hand, and put it between your legs."

I was helpless to deny him. When he commanded, my brain registered and obeyed. I kept my eyes on his and did as he said.

He pushed his thumbs into my heel and I arched again.

"Good. Now rub your clit until you shake, then sink those pretty fingers into your pussy. Show me how much you wish it was me touching you."

I rubbed a slow circle with my fingertip around the sensitive bundle of nerves. I was so needy from our encounters and all the tension that had been building over the past few days, hell, longer than that. Since I'd met both of them, the tension was always building.

He watched my ministrations and arched a brow. "You think I'd be gentle?"

My touch was timid. Slow. Two things Jack wasn't. He looked me in the eye, waiting for me to answer his question. A challenge. I knew as well as he that he wouldn't be gentle. He'd flick hard at my clit, then thrust two fingers into me, pumping in and out, deep and hard.

Just thinking about it made me pick up my pace. Just as my body picked up heat and I was on the brink of trembling, Cal walked in.

I removed my hand instantly, stopping in shock, and looked up at him. He just sank to his knees beside the tub, his forearms hanging over the edge to tap the water.

"Don't you dare stop," Jack rasped, completely ignoring Cal. But I couldn't ignore him, couldn't ignore the fact that I was giving myself an orgasm at Jack's command while Cal watched.

"Don't stop on my behalf, Kitten," Cal said with a look so fierce I couldn't do anything but lock my eyes on him and continue to rub.

"Inside," Cal said. "Bury that finger and think of me."

With a deep breath, I did. Sinking as far as I could go, my sheath gripped my finger and I arched into my own touch. The water sloshed around me, my nipples beaded with the cool air hitting them. They were standing up, begging for attention.

"Another finger," Jack said.

I withdrew completely, then returned with two. Slowly sinking back in. Then drug them out and sank again. Hitting deep. As deep as possible. A moan escaped my lips.

"You must be thinking of Cal," Jack growled, gauging the pace of my hand, he'd be right. "Now think of me."

I began thrusting faster. In and out until the water was swaying rapidly and my inner walls tensed as my hard, deep plunges increased to a rough pace. Jack. This was thinking of Jack. Rough and hard and fast. Then I'd slow for a moment. Keeping my fingers buried as deep as they could go, I pumped several times, not taking them from my body. Cal. Deep and consuming and close.

"Please," Cal whispered, as he leaned over the tub. "Your pretty nipples are begging to be sucked. Let me."

I moaned. I wanted that so much. The way his mouth felt on my skin haunted my dreams.

"Just . . . this . . . once . . . " I tried to stay in control, but that's all I could get out because I wanted that too. He didn't wait for more of an invitation. Instead, he snagged my pouting nipple between his lips and sucked hard.

"Oh, God, yes!" I arched further, silently begging him to take more. With Cal's mouth on my breasts, I pumped fast and hard.

I looked at Jack and his dark eyes were fixed on mine. He held my ankle tight, keeping me spread wide.

"Tell me," Jack said. "Tell me that you're going to come for me."

I nodded just as Cal bit the tip of my breast.

"Yes," I choked out, just as my orgasm took me over. I shuddered and spasmed so hard the water swished violently as my sheath clamped down on my fingers, shuddering and milking out my release over and over.

Jack growled in pleasure and Cal released my breast. They both stood. There, hovering over me as I breathed hard from the wicked pleasure.

"Jesus Christ. I'm going to need a fucking cold shower," Cal said, and turned to leave.

"I need a drink," Jack said, and was right behind him.

"Wait, you're leaving?" I called. They both paused and turned to look at me. What had happened? They were both there, had been a part of . . . whatever that was. And now were just walking out?

Cal's shoulders were tight and Jack was staring daggers at me. They looked uneasy. Like they didn't know how to process the moment we'd just shared, which was terrifying because I didn't know how to process it either. When it came to them, I responded. Now I was staring down a set of muscles and intensity and had no clue what to say.

"Good night, Lana," Jack said and left the room.

Cal scrubbed a hand down his face and looked at me once more. He almost said something, then stalled.

"See you in the morning," he finally decided to say. And sooner than they came, they went. I sat there, unable to call either one of them back.

Chapter 18

"Hey, I've missed you!" Harper's voice boomed through my phone. I sat on my bed and sighed at the instant happiness that flooded through me at hearing her voice.

"I've missed you too. How's your honeymoon?"

"Just got back. I'm telling you, the only way to spend Christmas is in Hawaii."

I smiled. That did sound nice. It was two days past Christmas now, and while she was back in the state, she was still further away than I needed for a hug.

"Tell me all about it," I asked.

"Well, hold on," she said. "I want to know what's going on with you. Rhett has gotten updates from the guys at the station. Apparently, Cal took time off, and no one has heard from him much."

"Yeah . . . um . . ." I glanced at my shut door. I'd spent the last day mostly locked in my room, trying to figure out how to act around the guys. I was also nervous and didn't trust myself entirely. "He's staying with me out in the middle of nowhere."

"Oh," Harper said. "I'm glad you got out of the dump hotel, but . . . are you okay?"

"Sort of," I said honestly. "The guys are treating me well, but it's tricky."

"Wait, guys? As in, both Jack and Cal are with you?"

"Yeah, it's their cabin. After you left, there was an incident and they basically stepped in and became my personal body guards."

"Yeah, I figured that, since last time I saw them they were parked outside your motel, but how is all that working? You're under the same roof with two of your exes."

Exes was a loose term, something I didn't really want to go into, since I had no idea what Cal and I or Jack and I were. We had history and feelings, both of which I was having a hard time getting a grip on.

"It's . . . challenging," I admitted.

"You can come stay with me," she said quickly. Harper was waiting on the insurance money just like I was, so I wasn't sure how or where she got a place. "I'm staying with Rhett in his ghetto one bedroom bachelor pad, but there's always room for you. Once the money comes in from the fire, then we're going to look at houses."

"That's great, Harp," I said, and felt truly happy for my best friend. "But I'm okay right now. Besides, I called the insurance company again. They assured me that they'd have a check for each of us within a week."

"Thank you for being so on top of everything," she said. "You sure you don't want to come here? The couch isn't much, but it's yours if you want it." I heard Harper giggle and what sounded like Rhett's voice in the background. A few kissing noises followed.

Though dealing with Jack and Cal was tricky, I didn't want to spoil Harper's newlywed bliss by crashing on her couch. I just had to make it a few more days. Once the New Year hit, things were looking up. I could go to the bank and see what was in this mystery lockbox, the insurance money would come in, and school was gearing up to start. My hope was that with the selling of my father's company, Anita would finally be off my back and the last tie I had with her and Brock would be severed.

Yeah, just a few more days. Then everything would be different. The only thing I didn't know about was how long the investigation would take for both my father's murder and the house fire. But so long as I got some sense of normalcy back, and the company was officially sold and Anita and Brock got their money, surely things would be better. They had to be. Because, even if Jack was right and they felt threatened by me or thought I had something to gain, that would all be put to rest with the company selling.

"You sure you're okay?" she asked. "I'm here if you need me."

"I know." And I did. I would be okay. Aside from this tension building, both sexual and otherwise. One thing I did need at the moment was advice. "Harper, I don't know what to do about Jack and Cal."

"They both want you bad, huh?"

I frowned. "Something like that. How did you know?"

"It was always obvious how they felt about you, so I'm not surprised. They are each so different, though."

Tell me about it. I had no idea where to start making sense of it all.

"The question is, though, do you want either of them?"

The truth was on my lips so quick I couldn't help but blurt it out. "Yes." I glanced around the room. Cal's room. "But it's not that simple. I can't choose. I love them both."

Even after making the decision to move past everything that had happened, the arrangement they'd made, I still loved them.

"Love sucks so bad sometimes," she said. "But it's also not easy or conventional or has a single path to get you there."

"I can't pick a path," I admitted. "I know I'll leave a mess when I go, and staying away from them is killing me as much as being with them is."

Harper let out a long breath. "I don't know what to tell you. If you can't choose, then walk away. Because stringing them along isn't good for anyone."

"I'm not stringing them along."

"I know. But you have an end date, right? You can't stay there forever."

I suppose I did. I hadn't marked it on the calendar or anything, but maybe a firm end date was a good idea.

"The second," I said. "I'm heading out the day after New Year's." Somehow, making a concrete statement twisted up my stomach. But I needed to have that end in sight. It was only then that I would be able to move past . . . everything. And Jack and Cal could move on too.

"Okay, then for the next few days, I'd take every moment, every opportunity you have to really see each of them. Maybe you'll find clarity and one will surpass the other and you'll know who it is you're meant to be with," Harper said.

"And, if I don't?"

"Then you're not out anything. You got to be with two people you care about and didn't want to choose between anyway. But take the time you have and use it to your advantage so you can walk away and be certain you made the right choice. Even if it means neither of them."

I closed my eyes, because deep down, I knew that the answer would remain me walking away from both. I couldn't imagine ever picking between one man who had my heart, and the other who had my soul.

Harper was right, I could use the time to be sure. Maybe then walking away wouldn't be as bad. I almost chuckled at the thought, because no matter what, it was going to be worse than bad. But denial had become my friend lately.

"If you change your mind, I'm here," Harper said. "The offer for the couch stands."

I laughed. "Thank you so much."

She laughed too and said, "Everything will work out how it's supposed to. I truly believe that."

Whatever Harper had gone through lately, with Rhett even, had her talking like a different person.

"I'm here for you too."

"I know. And once neither of us are technically homeless anymore, we're due for a girl's night and we'll catch each other up with everything."

"I'd like that." It was something normal to look forward to.

"Good luck, Lan," she said.

I hung up and took a deep breath, glancing at the door again. I'd need more than luck to face down what was on the other side of it.

I heard a crackling sound. Low, like a ghost's voice. An orange glow started to brighten as I stared off into blackness. The glow got bigger.

Pain and terror surged through me with every frantic breath. Fire.

What had been just a whisper was a scream now. Roaring

angry flames shot from every direction as I watched my house burn. Felt the heat on my face. The pain from where I'd been hit—

I gasped and shot up in bed.

Looking around, I lay in bed, coming down from the nightmare. From the reality that Brock and Anita were out there. Hating me. The person who started the fire was out there.

With several deep breaths, I got out of bed and looked out the window. I didn't remember falling asleep. But it was bright out, the morning giving way to the afternoon.

Even a cold shower didn't help the blistering fear I still felt from the dream. Felt from that night. When everything went up in flames around me. My house, my life, my love.

I thought about what Harper had said. I needed to be sure. Because my plan would be to walk away. There was no other way. Or maybe I was looking for excuses to be with them.

No.

I couldn't.

Shouldn't.

Despite everything, somewhere along the line, things shifted from getting away from them because they hurt me, to getting away from them because I was hurting them.

But I had some time. Time I should use wisely. I just had no idea how to do that.

There was no solution, which was something I was having a hard time stomaching. Because finding a solution was something I enjoyed. Weighing risk, smart decisions and statistics gave me control and a sense of normalcy.

Plugging Cal and Jack into a data system wouldn't work. Not this time.

Pulling on my jeans and T-shirt, I walked into the front room, hoping the universe would give me a sign. If there was a direction I was supposed to move, I needed to know now.

I entered the kitchen to see a shirtless and sweaty Cal bending over and rifling through the fridge.

Good God, the man was perfect. He stood, all that tan skin and those bulging muscles lightly misted with sheen from working out. At least, that was my guess. Since he wore a pair of low slung shorts and nothing else. Either way, I wasn't complaining.

"Emerged from the lair, huh?" he asked, turning to face me with a carton of orange juice in his hand.

"Lair? It's your room. I'm not the one who made it look like a cave."

He untwisted the carton top. "Cave is Jack's sense of design. Not mine."

I couldn't argue that. Cal's room reminded me of his house. Fresh and rugged and open. But still, he called it a lair. "The shower is made of stones. That's pretty cave-like if you ask me."

He took several swallows of the orange juice right from the carton until it was gone. I watched his ripped body flex and move, and I was certain watching him drink cold beverages could become a dangerous hobby. One I was ready to take on.

Nope. Focus. I needed to make a discernable effort and map feelings and moments and . . .

I blew out a breath.

I was trying to equate something that didn't have a quantifiable value. When Cal's blue eyes landed on me, I decided that there had to be a solution. Even if it was walking away.

"Normally, I'd be stoked to have you spending all this time in my room. Especially in my bed and my bathtub."

A flush pricked its way up my neck. I was crazy if I thought that incident wouldn't get brought up again. But Cal didn't push it. Instead, he tilted his head, examining me, and set the now-empty carton on the counter.

"I know a lot is wrong right now, and last night was," he paused. "Intense, so I won't ask that obvious question, but is there something extra wrong?"

I small grin tugged my lips like a puppeteer pulling a string. Cal had a way. A way to ask, a way to answer, a way to love. He made everything seem easy. He made me feel like if there were something "extra wrong" he would be there to help me deal with it.

Problem was, the extra wrong involved him. And Jack. And a future I couldn't face, but was trying to.

Collect data.

"Just thinking about a lot of things," I said, not wanting to go into my bad dream or the fact that, sure, someone setting fire to my home had a residual after-effect of making me feel scared. Like a target.

"What kind of things?" Cal asked. I caught the briefest twitch of his arm, as if he were going to reach out, but didn't. A loss flooded. He wasn't going to reach out for me. Because of my rule. Maybe because of something more than that. I knew how scary it was to reach out to someone.

"Things like the new year. Everything will change."

"Like?" he pressed.

His tone was quick and determined. Something I'd expect from Jack. But Cal had a serious side. A dark alpha side that always boiled beneath the surface.

I met his eyes. "Everything," I whispered.

He looked at me for a long moment as that one word hung heavy in the air like a piano on a string, slowly swaying back and forth. We both knew what it meant, but Cal seemed determined to cut the rope.

"Everything is very broad. Specify."

When I frowned at him, he just reached back and gripped the edge of the counter behind him. His rock hard abs, chest, and the sinful tattoo that lined it on full display and distracting as hell. But I kept my frown.

"Don't look at me like that. Jack's not the only one who wants answers." Determination coated the syllables. "You're not being a hundred percent honest. Tell me how you see things changing. And when."

I grappled for the will to steady my heart. "We're not going to stay in this cabin forever. Our time here will end."

"Thinking of the end now?" he challenged with a raised brow. I nodded. I couldn't tell if he was slightly playful or slightly terrified. "You obviously have a plan then?"

"The bank opens after New Year's Day."

"And if I say that I'll take you to the bank, figure out this lockbox issue, then bring you back here . . . ?" he waited for me to finish his sentence with an answer.

"I'd say no," I said softly.

So much silence passed between us that I started counting my heartbeats.

Boom-boom. Boom-boom.

The rhythm got louder the stiller Cal stayed.

Finally, he pushed off the counter and took a step toward me. He didn't stop himself from reaching out this time. He simply tucked a lock of hair behind my ear and said, "That doesn't give me much time to sway you then. Better bring out my A+ game."

I scoffed, but humor was lining the noise. He was likely thinking that he and Jack would do just that, sway me to stay. Like they had last time I'd brought up leaving. I couldn't bear to fight with him on this now. I'd set a hard date, but didn't want to have to actually defend that. It was too difficult.

"How do you feel about last night?" he asked. He'd said earlier it was intense, and that was definitely a way to describe it.

"It didn't feel wrong," I started. I'd been in the company of men I trusted. "But, afterwards, I didn't know how to feel or what to think."

"Me either," Cal admitted. "I knew I wanted you. Would do anything to have you. It didn't matter the circumstance. If you gave me an inch or a mile I would have taken it. But yeah . . . afterward . . . " He stroked my lock of hair again. "I didn't know what to do."

I glanced at his hand that was slowly running down my long hair.

"You never specified that I couldn't touch your hair. It's technically not touching *you*," he defended against the rule I didn't bring up.

"Uh-huh," I said with a sarcasm.

He stepped closer until I felt his warmth. Leaned into it even.

"Still not touching you," he said. While a hint of playfulness lined his voice, his gaze was anything but, and his mouth hovered closer to mine.

Boom-boom.

I could smell the sandalwood soap on his skin. So close I could almost taste it.

Boom-boom.

"Still not touching you," he whispered. He glanced from my lips to my eyes and finished with, "Unless you want me to . . . "

I breathed in everything he was and almost shook my head yes when a small voice in the back of my head whispered:

Are you ready to choose?

"I can't," I stuttered out, half in response to Cal and half to my own thoughts. If I couldn't choose, I couldn't close the distance.

I stepped back and Cal's fingers fell from the lock of my hair.

Breathing was proving difficult. I needed clarity. I didn't want to say goodbye to the kind of warmth Cal had. But I had to make some kind of effort to get a grip. I was supposed to be collecting data. See if one of the men passed the other. The notion seemed impossible, but I clung to Harper's advice. If I was going to walk away, alone or otherwise, I needed to be sure. And part of me did want to enjoy the little time I had. Because Cal was right. We didn't have a lot of time left. But contrary to what he thought, I was already swaying, between him and Jack.

"Lana?" Jack called from his room down the hall.

I closed my eyes for a moment, then opened them to find Cal's hadn't left my face. With a pathetic attempt for a smile, I excused myself from whatever moment I'd just missed with Cal and walked toward Jack.

"You beckoned?" I said, a little sharply, and stood in the doorway to his bedroom. Though it only looked half like a bedroom, the other side was dominated by an attached office. He had his own bathroom off to the left, but straight head, beyond the massive bed and rich dark colors, and a pile of blankets were on the floor, where I assumed Cal slept. Jack sat behind a large desk facing me.

Leave it to Jack to have an office everywhere he went.

"I want to discuss the logistics of going to the bank."

I crossed my arms and leaned against the door jamb. He watched my actions intently, then rose from behind his desk and walk around it.

"Please, come in," he offered like the invitation was a totally normal one. He sounded far too breezy. Like he was inviting me onto a sun porch. Not the bedroom of a man I had a hard time keeping my hands off of.

I took a step in, then another. He watched with what I could only describe as victory on his face.

"Why are you looking at me like that?" I asked, and took another step. Because, while I didn't exactly understand, I loved that look. That dark fire blazing behind his eyes was hard enough to handle, but this? This was deeper. It was the fire mixed with . . . joy.

"You coming toward me is the best sight in the world. I'm going to stare."

That made me stall. Not to upset him, but from shock. Jack was being painfully honest, something he'd done several times before, but this time? He looked like he really meant it. Like he'd rather watch me walk toward him than watch a sunset.

"You wanted to talk about the bank?" I reminded. Mostly for myself, because if he liked me walking toward him, he had no idea how much I wanted to run toward him as well. Then jump into his arms. And fall. Fall back into love the way we'd been. Fall over the edge of reason. Fall away from the world and get lost in the darkness of his eyes.

"Yes," he said quickly, glancing away for a moment, as if to clear his own head. "You wanted to go first thing when they opened, so we'll be leaving here early."

I nodded. I just had to make it two more days. A fact that both calmed and terrified me.

Two more days. That was it. The realization held a different tone in my head. One was celebratory and one was looming.

That. Was. It.

"Afterward," Jack continued, and my brain snapped to alert. I needed to be clear and honest now. And Jack was not going to like what I said next.

"No afterward," I cut in.

"Excuse me?" He took a step closer and I held my feet still, but my knees trembled. Not in fear of Jack, in fear of the future. Of the decisions I'd made and was set to make. Of the reality that the clock was ticking down and this feeling of Jack's presences engulfing me with every step would end.

"After the bank, I'm going my own way."

"And what way would that be?"

"I don't know," I said honestly. "But the money for my house should be in. I'll stay in a hotel until I find a place or—"

"You tried that already," Jack argued.

"Yes, and my plans were interrupted when you—"

"Stepped in because I was concerned about your safety? Took you away from that place after you and Bea were in an accident." He took another step. "That was me interrupting your plans, was it?"

"I know you're helping and care about my safety. And I've been scared, but I can handle it now."

"That's not all I care about, Lana," he said with a fierce tinge to his words. He looked at me like he was going to elaborate. I used that single second to pray to whatever power in the universe that he would. Instead, he cleared his throat and crossed his arms. "Nothing changes after the bank. You're still in danger."

"I think that everything will clear up after the company is sold."

"You're naïve."

That made ice prick my veins like freezing sharp points. "I'm not naïve. Eventually, I'll get in front of the judge with Brock. I just want my life back. I can't stay here for the rest of my days, trying to avoid you and Cal."

"First," he said, dropping his chin to look at me from beneath those dark brows. "You shouldn't be avoiding me. Cal, I'm fine with you avoiding, but not me." There was that cocky swagger I missed. "Second, I want you to have a life to go back to, which is why you'll stay with me."

"Jack, that's not going to happen."

"Give me a reason why."

"Because it'd kill me. Just this past week has been so hard. And I need to deal with things on my own. I appreciate everything you've done. I also don't appreciate a lot of things you've done, but this has an end date."

His eyes flared and I almost covered my mouth when my own words hit me.

This has an end date . . .

Jack had said something similar to me right before he left me. Crushing my world. What was worse was the expression on his face. Dark, dangerous, and pained.

"And you've had this end date in mind from the beginning?" he asked. And that was the blade in my gut that twisted. I may not have come up with the hard date until recently, but I'd known from the start this would all end. How things had changed. It was Jack on the other side of this conversation this time. I had to stand there and tell him . . .

"Yes. I've known from the beginning that this won't work." But last night confirmed it.

The ache redoubled, and I wondered for a moment if he felt this kind of stab when he'd said the same thing to me all those months ago. Did it matter? Maybe. Because this feeling was gutting. Especially when I had to stare down the man that had my heart and tell him I was walking away.

It's for the best.

Suddenly, my argument didn't hold water. Jack had said once that timing was everything. And I would have given everything for him to have stayed. Now, I was the one pulling away and all the reasons seemed second in comparison to remaining in his life, his arms, forever.

But I love Cal too . . .

I shook my head. Strength. Any of it I could call on, I did. I needed that will power now more than ever.

"Once the company is sold, there will be no more ties to Anita or Brock," I said. Despite Jack's words, I wasn't naïve enough to think that the fire to my house or my father's death didn't matter and those two VanBurens didn't know something about either. Hopefully, they'd be happy to have nothing between us, and while I waited for the burden of proof to show up, I'd have to be okay with taking care of myself. Now I just had to convey that to Jack.

"I'll be okay. I'll find a place, have an alarm installed. School starts soon, and that will keep me busy."

I was listing things like it was necessary to convince myself, and Jack, why this was going to happen. But the excuses fell short. The truth was, it didn't have anything to do with my safety. It had to do with Jack and Cal.

"I won't allow this," Jack said in a deep, menacing voice.

"You don't have a choice. It's what I'm doing."

He grinned, but there was nothing light about it. "Oh, I have a choice," he said with salt. "Just like you have a choice to carry out this little plan of yours. You want your life back? Fine. Have it. But don't think I won't be there." Another step. "Because *you* are *my* life, Lana. And I want it back too."

My chest snapped in half like a wooden pencil. My ribs couldn't handle the pressure his words delivered.

He stopped so close that all I saw was his chest. He gathered my hair in his hand, wrapped some of it in his fist, and yanked enough to bring my chin up to have my gaze meet his. The slight sting of his grip sent shivers to every part of my body. His touch, his pull, was perfection. Even when he was right in front of me, I craved more.

"Cal got to touch your hair, so I assume this doesn't violate your rules," he rasped. That sneaky man. He'd must have seen Cal and me in the kitchen, then purposefully went back to his office to call me.

I narrowed my glare on him. He obviously knew I'd figured out his maneuver. My gaze went from his eyes to his mouth, and I was going to give in any second. I needed to get away. I needed to stay.

I couldn't do either.

"I need . . . " I looked into his eyes again, and wanted to finish that sentence in so many ways. Instead, I went with, "paper."

He frowned and took a step back. Letting my hair fall from his fist.

I righted myself on a shaky breath and clarified. "And a pen please."

Jack walked to his desk and gave me a legal pad and pen. I grabbed them quickly and left.

It was time I followed through.

Chapter 19

He makes me feel confident . . .

He makes me feel strong . . .

He makes me feel safe . . .

He makes me feel seen . . .

"Damn it," I muttered, and scribbled another line on the legal pad. I'd spent the last day locked away in my room, writing. Lists. Ideas. Pros and cons. Nothing was getting me anywhere.

I looked at the pages and pages of my thoughts on paper, and one stood out and almost hurt to look at:

JACK VS. CAL.

They each had a column. Despite my best efforts and all the differences that were evitable between them, I was stuck, a dead line down the middle, neither of them edging in front.

There was no choice to make.

I knew it. Had known it the whole time. But I'd tried in every way I knew how – right down to listing their attributes – to see if there was any hope. All that'd been accomplished was making the obvious more clear. And the one thing I'd known all along remained: I can't choose.

I tossed the legal pad on the bed next to me and let out a long breath. It was New Year's Eve, the brink of a fresh start, and yet I felt anything but relieved. Yes, this year was almost done, and what a year it'd been. And with the new beginning ringing in at midnight, that fresh start I was counting on was daunting. Because I'd be facing every day after with the realization of what love, lust, and happiness were, but not have them.

I looked around the four walls that had been my hiding place. Maybe Cal was right. Maybe this was a lair. But it was time to get out of it. The running shoes Cal had gotten me sat on the chair in the far corner. It was time for a different approach, time to get out of the corner and run.

Quickly throwing on leggings and a sweatshirt, I tied the sneakers and walked into the front room, where I was greeted by two large men.

"Going somewhere?" Cal asked, taking in my attire.

"The answer should be no," Jack said, keeping his eyes on me.

"Actually, I was going to go for a jog."

"No," Jack said again, only more slowly this time, like it was the only word in his vocabulary.

"You can't keep me here," I said, and his dark eyes lit up as if excited for a challenge.

But Cal stood up and smiled.

"Can too," Cal said with a grin and held out his arms. "Look how big I am."

Jack didn't seem amused, but I kind of was. Cal broke the tension and I headed toward the door.

"The sun is already setting," Jack said.

"Then I better hurry if I'm to make my curfew," I replied with mock politeness.

"If you think that mouth of yours and this challenging

disposition isn't going to come back to bite you, you're sorely mistaken," Jack said and got really, really close. "And I *will* bite you, baby. And I'll enjoy every minute."

That made my breath stall.

When he stood to his full height, I saw Cal right behind him, slipping his shoes on.

"What are you doing?"

"Going for a run with you." He tossed me a smile. "Jack will be happy that you're not out alone, and I will be happy because our runs through the woods typically turn eventful."

"Oh, no, no way," I said. "I'm going to get some air and some space, and you two are just going to sit here and deal with it."

Cal frowned. "You can't go by yourself. It's dangerous."

Good Lord, there was no winning. "I was going to go along the road." Which had no cars, since we were in the middle of nowhere, but I could keep track of where I was and how to get back. Not that I was going to throw them a bone.

"If you don't want Cal to go with you, I will," Jack said.

"I want to go by myself."

They both looked at me like they didn't understand the word, and part of my heart drooped a little. Every expression that hit Cal's face was a battle. His body was practically humming to chase me. I saw it from the glint in his eyes to the disappointment set in his mouth. Because, yeah, our runs did turn eventful. Something I couldn't get out of my memory, even if I wanted to. But I needed to think, an honest deep breath, and last ditch effort to decide how to spend what would be a brand new year come a few hours from now.

Jack just looked pissed. Not that I was being challenging, but because he held his tongue and didn't challenge back. He looked like he was . . . stuck. Stuck in his mind. Stuck trying to figure out the best way to handle this situation.

"You'll come back," he said. But if I wasn't paying attention, it almost sounded like a question. Jack's eyes held a hint of fear that I may just not.

"Yes," I said softly. "I'm coming back. I just need some air."

"Okay."

My eyes shot up. Okay? Jack looked tortured, but he uttered the one word he seemed disgusted with.

"You make it seem like I'm asking for a lot. I'm just taking a short jog."

Jack nodded once. "I know. But watching you walk away is asking me to handle a lot."

I swallowed hard. "Trust me, I know the feeling."

That may have been a cheap shot, and it showed on the harsh plains of Jack's brow. I wish I could pull it back, but it was said. The truth. Watching him leave that day had changed everything. And it hurt. He'd walked out on me, I'd walked out on Cal, and now I was running from both of them. But there was one thing that was different.

"I'll be back shortly," I whispered, and Jack's eyes met mine. I looked at him for a moment, then turned to Cal who seemed just as uneasy as Jack.

With that, I opened the door, and walked out.

The snow crunched beneath my feet. I'd decided that a brisk walk was more in line than a jog. Running in snow was tricky and I'd almost slipped twice. But I was heading back up the road now and toward the cabin.

The last signs of the sun were diminishing quickly, and the night was graying by the second. The air did nothing for my mind. The New Year would be ushered in tonight, and with that the promise of the future I had no clue about. It was like starting over in the dark after experiencing the light.

My breath fogged around me and the cabin came into view as I wound around the small road.

A loud shot fired and I jumped. Several birds flew to the sky in a scattered cluster.

A gunshot . . .

It fired again, this time closer.

I screamed. Bone chilling fear slapped my body all at once. They'd found me. Wanted me dead. I should have known better. I was easy pickings, just like I had been when I was young. Brock sitting back and waiting, keeping me on the verge of fear until he decided to attack.

I ran as fast as I could, my heart beating so loud it was pounding in my ears like a drumline. I sprinted faster, not caring that the snow was getting thicker as I got near the edge of the road.

Another shot rang out.

I tried to stay focused and just run. The snow around my ankles got thicker and gripped me like the cold terror surging through my blood. I kept my eyes on the front door. Almost there . . .

Jack and Cal both rushed out of the cabin, and I saw them both see me just as I came up on the house. Jack's eyes met mine for a brief moment. "Are you hurt?" he yelled loudly.

"No." I was just terrified.

He then he took off running in the direction I'd come from, right as I launched myself into Cal's open arms.

"Gunshots," I said against his warm chest. "Don't," I called after Jack, realizing he was bounding *toward* the danger. I tried to stop Jack, but Cal was pushing and pulling at my clothing.

"Are you hit?" he asked frantically.

"I'm fine," I told him, but he kept searching my entire body, as if he had to see for himself that I was really okay. "I'm just scared."

That got through to him and his hands slowed. He wrapped me in his strong arms and pulled me closer. He kissed me hard. His eyes were squeezed shut with worry. He pulled away to whisper, "Come on, let's get you inside."

I shook my head and yanked away. "Not without Jack. What is he doing? Jack!" I called again. But he was already around the corner and out of sight.

"He's going to find who shot the gun," Cal said, keeping his big body in front of mine as if he were my own personal shield.

"They have a gun! He could get killed!"

I stepped Jack's direction, trying to get around Cal, but he wouldn't let me. "He'll be fine. Inside, Lana."

Cal looked like he was about to throw me over his shoulder himself and haul me in when Jack reappeared around the corner and bounded toward us.

"Hunters," he breathed hard, not slowing his stride or taking his eyes off me. "Saw them over the ridge."

I swallowed hard. "S-so I'm safe?"

Jack's dark eyes turned fierce. "Not from me."

He didn't stop until his body was against mine. Cupping my face, he kissed me hard, and I felt all the tension and relief surge through him. The same emotions hit me. Fear and happiness. I was so scared. And I'd run. Not just away, but toward the two men I loved.

"I was so scared," I said against Jack's mouth.

"So was I, baby," he kissed me hard, sucking my bottom lip between his to pull me even closer and devour my mouth like I was his own personal oxygen source. I squeezed my eyes tight. Every rule, every reasonable thought, faded away.

Keeping his demanding mouth on mine, he backed me up until I hit a large, warm wall of muscle. Cal. He was right behind me. He was comforting and safe and right there with me. They both were.

I tried to match Jack's powerful mouth. Using all the adrenaline I had, I wove my tongue with his while reaching back for Cal. I needed to feel him too. Thankfully, he didn't pull away, his big hands cupped my hips and pulled me back against his chest further. Surrounded. I was completely caged by the two men that drove me to the brink of insanity.

Pure instinct drove every short-circuiting nerve ending.

I broke from Jack long enough for Cal to turn me in his arms and take my mouth with his.

"I won't let anyone hurt you," he whispered, then kissed me deeply. I couldn't find my feet because both men, both kisses, felt right.

Cal was just as commanding, but with deliberate slowness. Taking an extra second in every move of his strong jaw. Like he was crazed, yet savoring every taste. He took me through the doorway and Jack was at my back. The door shut behind us and the warmth of indoors hit my body hard.

The sound of fire crackling in the hearth and heat radiating only grew, as Cal and Jack seamlessly worked together to maneuver me in front of the fireplace. I felt them both. Hands and mouths brushing over my whole body until I felt touched everywhere at the same time.

Cal continued to ravage my mouth, surging his tongue deep the way he would make love to me, and I was lost to it.

Then, Jack's hand was at my back, lifting my shirt to my

shoulders and kissing along my lower back. Hot hands, mouths, were everywhere and I couldn't think. Couldn't breathe. Just wanted to get lost. To feel their love.

When Cal leaned back, releasing my lips, I had one second to take in air. Jack took the opportunity to lift my shirt over my head so fast I barely registered it happened. With a snap of his wrist, by bra was undone and sliding down my arms, ready to fall.

There wasn't time to think, all I could do was feel, and this felt right. Deep down in my heart and soul, this felt so incredibly right I felt everything else slide away. All of the fears and the past and the choices disappeared and left this one moment.

These two men.

And I was a goner. My body relaxed like a weight was physically being lifted from it. Fear and stress were replaced with a sense of need. The need to stay. With them.

Jack kissed my lips softer than he ever had and a spark hit my stomach. But before it flared into full ignition, he pulled back. With a tight grip on my hips, he spun me back to face Cal.

Cal smiled and snagged my lips with his. Another soft taking, like a whisper or a plea for me to stay. My body recognized what pleasure I was skating around and wanted it so much.

The internal switch that had guided me from day one, flipped on. All I wanted was to feel. Touch. Experience.

Them.

I knew the moment Cal felt my agreement. Because his kissed deepened and my hands wandered. Fingertips itching for the need to feel skin. I tugged at his shirt. He pulled it off, straying from my mouth for only a moment to do so. He pulled my bra the rest of the way down my arms and off, and while his mouth devoured mine, Jack wrapped my hair around his fist and bit down on the back of my neck.

I gasped into Cal's mouth. A gasp Jack made me feel, yet Cal was there to catch it.

Emotions skyrocketed and my body flared further. I couldn't focus on anything but the feel of Cal's warmth and Jack's heat.

I reached behind me to blindly claw at Jack's pants. Fast. Touching them, pulling at the material that covered them, it was all fast. My hands worked with intent, unhooking Cal's belt, then yanking open Jack's button up.

With their help, both kicked away their clothing and my hands could finally do what they wanted. Feel their skin.

When Jack pressed against my back and Cal against my front, I felt their bare skin from both directions, and it was like floating in my own cloud of bliss. I closed my eyes for a moment, worried that if I opened them, I may realize this was a dream.

My pulse was ready to sprint right out of my chest and I needed more. The feel of Cal's hard cock pressing into my stomach and Jack . . .

I wiggled a little to feel him behind me. His strong body was firm against mine and his heavy erection prodded at the small of my back. They were both naked. Ready. And the only desire that read clear in the haze of my mind was *more*.

As if reading my face, Cal said, "Don't worry. I'm going to give you exactly what you want. Nice and slow."

His lips skimmed down my neck to my breasts, and he knelt before me. I gripped the top of his head for balance, as he helped me out of my shoes and pants. When they were discarded, he looked up, a wild fire haloing him, making his blond stubble dance like flecks of gold on his face. He was beautiful. I couldn't help but trail my fingers along his strong jaw while his dazzling gaze looked up at me.

Jack's strong arm wrapped around my waist and the hand in

my hair tugged, thrusting my chin in the air so he could kiss my jaw. The instant sting of his dominance sent tremors from my scalp to my core.

"Speak for yourself," Jack said and ran his teeth along my jaw. "I'm going to take you hard and fast. Just like you like it, don't you, baby?"

I nodded. Then I wanted to shake my head. Because I liked both.

Cal didn't stand. Instead, Jack maneuvered himself and me to our knees to meet Cal on the plush rug. The fire burned bright and heated my skin, but both men put those flames to shame.

"Can you trust me?" Jack said finally, his hand unwrapping from my hair.

I looked at Cal in front of me and answered Jack's question. "Yes."

Because I did. I trusted both of them so much. Loved them so much. Whatever part of my brain that knew this was a bad idea shut down. I wanted to stay in the moment. I didn't want to run or hide. I wanted the men that taught me how to do both.

"Come here," Jack said, adjusting me so I sat on my bottom and leaned back against him, like he was my own personal recliner. I lifted my head just enough to kiss along his neck and jaw. His olive skin and short stubble felt like sandpaper against my mouth. It scratched in the best way and made my lips pulse hard from the small scrape.

"Do not take your mouth from me," Jack rasped in my ear and both his hands reached down to grab my thighs. "Do you understand?" I nodded and gave another kiss to his neck. He growled and yanked my legs apart.

I gasped and my attention snapped to Cal, who was kneeling in front of me and staring between my legs like a lust-crazed animal. But Jack's hand was already covering me, and moving in fast circles over my heat.

"Do you have any idea what you do to me?" Jack growled in my ear. He moved his hand from between my legs to my lips. I sucked them. "Every sexy little noise you make and every ounce of passion you have is a fucking drug to me."

Cal took the opportunity to sink between my legs. I jolted with a surge of need when I felt his teeth graze the fleshy part of my inner thigh as he traveled higher.

Jack moved his neck, running his chin along the side of my cheek, reminding me of his demand. While Cal's mouth was on me, I had to keep mine on Jack.

I leaned back a little more. Jack cupped my throat and turned my face up so I could easily sample the flavor of his skin and nibble his neck.

It was hard to concentrate on anything. From the corner of my eye, I saw Cal hover over the aching heat between my legs. He flicked the little bundle of nerves once and I moaned and sank back into Jack's strong hold even more.

"Best treat on earth," Cal rasped, then licked the length of my entire sex.

"Oh, God," I whispered.

Jack's cock pressed so hard against my back and I squirmed a little thinking of it. Of him. Wanting to be filled.

Cal licked again, dipping his tongue inside for one long thrust. I gasped, breathing in Jack's scent as Cal stayed deep, flicking and moving his tongue in a way that hit every nerve ending, and then some.

He pulled out, then thrust in again, the wicked way he was tasting sent electric chills to the surface of my skin, pricking my nipples and tightening them into hard points. Jack's palms were right there to deliver the perfect amount of pressure to my aching breasts.

Cal moaned, like devouring me was the best thing in his world. And, God, I wanted to be that for him so much. He retreated, then surrounded my swollen clit with his lips and sucked.

I jolted again, Jack's firm grip catching me. I arched my back and threw out my hips, rocking into Cal's waiting mouth.

"She wants more," Jack rasped.

"Oh, I know she does," Cal groaned. "She's already drenching my tongue. Best fucking honey I've ever tasted." Cal took another sample. Slow. So painfully slow that I thought my body would melt into a puddle. But Jack surrounded me. Somewhere in the back of my foggy brain, I liked it. Liked it so much that for this moment, we were all there. No choice. No future. No consequence. Just us. All of us.

Jack growled in my ear. "I know how good you taste," he said. "But I want you to refresh my memory."

I nodded shakily and reach down between my legs like he'd done earlier. Cal kissed my inner thigh, allowing me access to dip my fingertip inside my opening. Cal was right. I was so ready. So turned on that I was beyond wet. I lifted my newly wetted finger to Jack and he sucked it into his mouth and groaned.

"Fuck, you're delicious." He sucked once more until he'd cleaned my finger and pinched the peaks of my breasts hard while Cal delivered kisses along my thighs. Jack's rough sting and Cal's slow seduction were trapping every ounce of pleasure and keeping it hostage.

Jack's pinch turned to a roughened massage.

"I could eat you for every meal," Cal said.

Jack bent enough to snag my lips in his teeth and kissed me

hard. His tight grip on my breasts sent shock waves through my system.

Cal drove his tongue back inside of me, and I couldn't hold back. He ate at me like an ice cream cone that was melting in the sun. Because that's what I was doing. Melting.

"Need more," Cal said and tossed my legs over his shoulders and yanked me up to meet his mouth. The action sent me sliding down Jack's hard body, until my head rested in his lap.

Cal's tongue danced like a master over my entire core. Every time he brushed over my opening, my hips instantly reached out, taking his tongue deep for a single inward glide before he retreated to suck my clit.

Rocking and moving, so in sync it drove me mindless.

I tensed so hard with the need to let every ounce of pleasure take over. I missed Jack's touch, his kiss. With my cheek resting on his thigh, I was eye level with his hard cock.

He told me not to take my mouth from him . . .

I flicked my tongue out to taste his impressive shaft. He was hot and velvety, and that internal switch notched up into overdrive. I needed more, but I couldn't move enough to suck him deep. So I licked the side of his shaft, sucked the outside of the crown, and ran my tongue along the length.

Jack hissed a breath and wove his fingers through my hair.

"More," I begged. I wanted to take him deep into my mouth, but couldn't. So I sucked the side of his cock again. Just then, Cal sank two large fingers into me and I gasped.

"Give her whatever she wants," Cal rasped. "She's close."

Jack moved from behind me and knelt beside me. I sat up, supporting my weight on my straightened arms behind me. He palmed the back of my head and gripped his cock in his other hand.

"You really want more?" Jack asked, running the tip of his cock along my bottom lip. I knew he was waiting for me to look at him and say it. To beg for it.

"Yes, please. I need more."

With that, he shoved his cock between my lips and I sucked greedily. With Cal between my legs, lighting up magic with every sweep of his tongue, I was so close to an ecstasy I didn't know existed. I felt whole for the first time in a very long time. Because I had them both.

Cal thrust his tongue deep inside me just as Jack plunged into my mouth. I had them both. Felt them both. And the crackling fireworks couldn't be denied.

My body shuddered, and with a bolt of lightning, both Jack and Cal buried deep. Ice and fire took turns pouring through my system as my body exploded with white hot and red cold tremors. I came harder than I ever had. I moaned loudly, the vibrations surrounded Jack's shaft in my mouth and my hips bucked against Cal.

"Good girl," Jack praised. His stomach muscles tightened and all those amazing ab muscles flexed. He pulled away, but kept my head in his hand for support, a welcome thing because my orgasm wouldn't stop.

Cal buried his fingers deep and kept them there, pumping hard without retreating while licking my clit madly.

"Keep coming, Kitten," he rasped between licks. "I'm not near done with you."

Jack bent and sucked my nipple. The feel of wet suction kicked off another set of shivers. I screamed to the ceiling, breathing hard, falling and shattering into a thousand pieces, only to be swept up and those piece flung back into the air like graffiti again.

"Cal," I called out for him. I needed to feel his skin, his strength. When his fingers left me and he sat back, I launched myself at him. He wrapped me up instantly and kissed me hard. But I was too crazed for slow. Too gone for soft. I licked down his neck to his chest and took big bites of his hard muscles, then traced his tattoo with my tongue. Both his hands threaded into my hair and his head dropped back. I felt his heartbeat kick up from beneath my lips.

I didn't stop. Couldn't. I licked down his abs. Those steely muscles hardening further beneath my tongue until I thought they'd rip through his skin. He stayed still, kneeling in front of me and letting me love on him.

Just as I nibbled on his hip bone, I blindly reached back for Jack. He gripped my hand. He was there. They both were there. But that hand slipped from mine and Jack positioned himself behind me, helping me to my hands and knees. He kissed and bit my ass, and then I felt his hard cock drag over the back of my thigh.

"You want me, baby?" Jack asked. The hot head of his shaft prodded my opening. "Your sweet little pussy is weeping." He pushed just the tip in, then retreated, and I wanted to scream from the distance. "Who are you begging for?"

"Both of you," I said with all the truth in the world.

I licked and laved at Cal's cock like I would his mouth. Tasting and devouring. He groaned. Jack smacked my ass and I gasped.

"She's getting wetter," Jack said, rubbing my ass where he'd just spanked it.

Cal smiled down at me. "Tell him why, Kitten. Tell him why you're hot and dripping."

"B-because I like tasting you."

"Anything else?" Jack asked, as he delivered another smack on my bottom. I moaned, sucking Cal deep as my inner walls spasmed on the brink of another orgasm. Jack's sinful touch lit up the darkest parts of my desires like nothing else could.

"I love you touching me. Hard. Sharp ..." I pushed back against Jack, trying to coax him inside, but he held me still.

I ran my tongue along the crown of Cal's impressive cock and the grip in my hair tightened.

"Good. Because you're going to get that *more* you want so bad."

I sucked Cal deep, just as I felt Jack surge into me.

I screamed in pleasure, but Cal's thick shaft buried in my mouth cut off the noise.

"You're perfect," Jack growled. He pulled out quickly, then thrust back inside all the way to the hilt. He took me so hard, so thoroughly that I rocked forward, taking Cal's cock even deeper into my throat.

With a tight hold on my hips, Jack fucked me hard, slamming me back into his waiting length over and over, pulling almost all the way out before he hammered back home again. Our skin slapping and his fingers digging into my skin were sounds and feelings that awoke every sense I had. He knew how to work my body over. Knew how to deliver every ounce of pleasure in a rough, consuming way until I was begging. Begging to come. Begging for it to never end.

I sucked hard on Cal and he groaned.

"Jesus, you're so damn good," he said. I looked up at him and the wicked blue heat in his eyes was my undoing. With him deep in my throat and Jack pounding hard from behind, a shocking release hit me again.

Cal just stared at me, and I couldn't take my eyes off of him. The first dose of pleasure was lightning, this was thunder.

Booming and clapping through my veins so loudly I had to squeeze my eyes shut from the intensity.

"Best fucking thing I've ever seen," Cal said and slipped out of my mouth. He was breathing hard, that meaty chest rising and falling rapidly. He looked so close to coming that his cock looked angry. I'd never seen it that big.

"Lift up," Cal coaxed softly.

Jack buried himself to the hilt, fitting snuggly in my depths, then pulled me back until my shoulders met his chest, helping me carry out Cal's request.

Cal instantly latched onto my nipple and took a deep draw. My head fell back to rest on Jack's shoulder. Nothing had ever felt this good. I was being cherished, by two men.

My skin didn't know which pleasure point to respond to first. Because with Jack nestled deep inside me and Cal sucking at the sensitive peaks of my breasts, I was in a constant state of delirium. The buzzing of release was never far away, and I gave myself over to it. I let the feel and taste of them sweep me up and take me.

Cal gripped my sides and lifted me away from Jack.

Jack slipped from my body and Cal laid me flat on my back. The plush carpet tickled my shoulders. Cal didn't waste any time. He opened my legs wide and in one long thrust, sank deep into my depths.

I arched and staggered on a harsh inhale. Staying deep, he surged his hips forward again and again, stirring slow and never leaving my body. Pressure built from the sensitive spot he hit inside. With every insistent twist of his hips, his cock touched a spot that sent my blood to liquid fire and my breasts bobbed with each thrust he delivered.

Jack snagged a nipple between his teeth and gently bit. I

reached for him. His dark hair was soft as I wound my fingers through it. He sucked and ate at my breasts like a starving lion, and I arched further into his mouth while Cal continued his deep thrusts.

"Come again," Cal said. "I want to feel it around my cock this time."

Jack's hand slid down my stomach and found the swollen bundle of nerves. He rubbed fast circles over and over as Cal continued pumping.

"Oh, God . . . please."

I didn't know if I was begging to come again or begging for oblivion because whatever I was falling over, I didn't think I'd be able to come back from. They were working my body over. Using every one of my pressure points against me and I loved every second.

I found Cal's wild blue gaze and tried to breathe. But I couldn't. Between Jack's hard sucking at my breast, fingers working fast, and Cal's deep penetration, I was flying through the air with no ground in sight.

"That's it," Cal said and thrust hard. I watched his muscles bunch tighter as he did it again and again. "I feel you gripping me." Thrust. "You like it deep?"

I nodded spastically.

Cal's face was set with lust and awe. "Then show me. Show me how much you like it."

My body didn't match up with my words because none came. But that's exactly what my body did. In a wild intense release I couldn't stop. Over and over, my inner walls shuddered and I sobbed to the ceiling from the overpowering ecstasy.

With a final pinch of my clit, Jack moved away. My orgasm was still going when Cal's release caught him. His whole body vibrated, but those steely blue eyes stayed on mine. On a final thrust, he flexed his hips, hitting the edge of my sanity before he pulled away. I didn't have time to breathe, to think. Jack's hand was on my knee in an instant, and he tugged me toward him and thrust deep into my core.

I gasped and choked at the sudden invasion. It was a blissful surprise. He fucked me impossibly hard and fast. Five, six, seven deep pumps, then with those blazing onyx eyes wrapped around me, he came hard.

I felt every twitch of his muscle and the final a surge of pleasure that never dissipated crept through my veins, making me tremble. I trembled from exhausted happiness. I closed my eyes for a moment. Feeling everything. But in one slide, Jack pulled away.

I opened my eyes to find two very strong, very tall men on their knees in front of me, breathing hard and looking like they both were ready to either throttle me or kiss me.

Hot, raw, angry lust surrounded the three of us. Surrounded them. And I had no idea what to do. How to feel. Other than higher than any drug could ever take me.

But, like any drug, there would be a crash. And this time it would be hard.

Chapter 20

I splashed some water on my face and patted it dry with a towel. The pink pajamas Jack had brought me felt extra soft against my skin. Or maybe it was that my skin was extra sensitized. Only moments ago, I'd had two men paying every inch of me a lot of attention. And now, standing in the bathroom, I felt alive and flecks of hope ran through my veins like shards of silver.

It was officially the New Year. A chance to start fresh. And what had happened in the living room between the two men I loved and me, was something I never saw coming. But it left my body, mind, and soul at odds.

I walked out of that bathroom and stopped immediately.

"Hey," I said, looking between Jack and Cal, who stood almost shoulder to shoulder and stared me down. They both were in low slung pajama pants. Jacks were black and Cal's were red. I tried not to get distracted by their hard upper bodies. Especially when Jack crossed his arms and stared me down.

Something had shifted. Clearly, I had missed a conversation, because Jack looked pissed and Cal just looked irritated.

"What's wrong?" I asked.

Cal shook his head. But Jack was quick to answer my question. "I noticed you came in here."

"Yeah. I was getting ready for bed." I knew we'd end up discussing what had just happened, but Jack's line of questioning was throwing me.

"In here," Jack snapped. It wasn't a question, but I took it as one.

"Yes. This is my room."

"No, this is Cal's room," Jack corrected quickly, the sharp edge to his voice cutting through the air and striking my chest.

"You're making a big deal out of nothing," Cal said to Jack.

Yep, I had missed something. And apparently it involved my presence in Cal's room.

"Really?" Jack eyed Cal. "If it's no big deal, then you wouldn't mind if I took Lana to *my* room?"

Cal's nostrils flared and a flash of pure rage settled over his scarily still frame. He looked ready to kill. Something Jack seemed to notice as well. But Jack just scoffed and grinned like he'd won an argument.

"That's what I thought," Jack said. "So don't tell me this isn't a big deal because she's in your bed and not mine. You know what that would do to you?"

I closed my eyes. Whatever amazing moment we'd all just shared was now getting drowned out by the weight of the aftermath. There was only one of me, and while I'd tried to stick to my own rules, I'd failed. And now the competition was back.

"She's been in here the whole week," Cal said, squaring his shoulders to face Jack. "She's not going anywhere."

Jack took a step toward Cal. "We'll see about that."

"Stop," I said. They both looked at me. "What is going on?

202

What has changed? Why is this room situation suddenly a problem?"

"What's changed?" Jack asked, like it was the dumbest question on earth. Which it kind of was. I knew that the moment I'd committed to both of them. And Jack was livid. "What changed is what just happened in the living room," he snapped.

I glanced down.

"Don't you dare," Jack said. "Don't look away now."

I found his dark gaze and bit the inside of my lip to keep it from trembling. This was bad. Everything in my gut was telling me that we were all standing on the brink of a jagged cliff and any moment we'd fall. And we'd get cut up on the way down.

"I didn't mean to . . . " I stopped because I had no idea how to finish that sentence. Truth was, I had meant to continue. With both of them. Because I had the chance to feel them. To love them. Without having to pick. And it was the most amazingly beautiful moment of my life. But this moment would make or break everything. And we all knew it.

Cal's eyes were shimmering with wild caged beasts behind those blues.

"I don't want to ruin everything," I said honestly.

"That's what's happening," Jack replied. "The only way for everything not to be ruined is for you to choose."

My mouth parted and a painful gust of air stuck to my throat.

"I can't," I whispered.

"Lana," Cal's voice was terrifyingly low. "I don't know what the hell to do." He threaded his fingers together and placed them on the top of his head, then looked at the ceiling as if hoping for an answer. "What happened out there . . . I was caught up. I want you so damn much that I just shared you with my best friend."

He sounded concerned for me. I didn't know how to fix that, other than to tell the truth.

"I liked every second of what we shared tonight," I said.

"Which *we* are you talking about?" Jack asked.

"Both of you . . . all of us," I clarified.

"I don't know what to do with that," Jack said, seeming just as lost as Cal. "All of us doesn't really work."

And that was on my shoulders. I knew them. Knew they each needed control. Knew they couldn't be second in any way, to me or one another. And I just gave in to the passion and selfishly wanted both of them.

Jack hovered near my bed, pacing around the side, looking at the mattress. He stopped suddenly and without turning to look at me said, "Choose."

Ferocity dried out that single word.

I looked at Cal for support, but he just nodded.

"Jack's right. You need to choose."

My vision was narrowing, like a tunnel was closing in. Neither of them had come out and demanded my choice before. I'd been clear from the start that I wouldn't choose, but this? The ultimatum? My chest tingled, trying to call on that numbness I'd gotten so good at implementing. But it didn't come. Deep down, I was on the cusp of losing everything, and I knew it. And my body was forcing me to feel the ache of that coating my stomach.

"But, just a moment ago, you said I didn't have to choose," I whispered.

Jack's dark eyes settled on mine. "That moment is over. Things changed."

It hurt to swallow those words down. It wasn't about the room. It wasn't about where I'd sleep, it was about what each room represented. Them. Jack was right, everything had changed the moment I reached out for both of them. And I was stupid enough to think that hope had anywhere to thrive.

"Can we talk about this some more?" I asked. Maybe we could find some middle ground or at least get all our emotions out. It was a new, difficult position to be in, after having just shared so much.

"No," Jack said with so much anger I didn't know what to say. Jack faced me once more and Cal took a moment to pace himself. This was beyond any "normal" situation, but I couldn't face the truth that I was staring down the single moment I'd been avoiding for a long time.

Choice.

"I can't choose between you two."

"Why?" Cal said, his own snap having extra heat behind it. "Why, Lana?" He pressed harder. "Why can't you just say who you want? Deep down, you must know."

"She does," Jack said, and my gaze shot to his. "She's been comparing us. Listing our qualities."

The walls felt like they were closing in on me. I glanced at the bed where I'd left the legal pad. All my notes and lists . . . that's what Jack had just been looking at. It looked bad. Really, really bad, but I could explain—

"Did you know our little Lana here gets different things from each of us?" Though Jack was talking to Cal, he kept his eyes on me. My heart was going to beat out of my chest.

"What the hell are you talking about?" Cal asked, glancing between the two of us.

"I'm talking about the way you make her feel safe," Jack said. "And I give you . . . what was it?" He tilted his head to the side, but I knew there was nothing wrong with his memory. He'd clearly read what I'd written down and was now pulling out every weapon he had to play. "Ah, yes, I give you strength."

Too bad I didn't feel strong. Not in the least. Every hard look, every word spoken, was another bullet loaded to the chamber.

"Check the notepad," Jack motioned to the bed and Cal saw it right away. "You were trying to choose," Jack continued. "Otherwise, you wouldn't have made a list comparing *every single moment* we shared with another."

Another bullet loaded.

Raw hurt and anger were humming off of Jack. And Cal appeared to have been hit with the gravity of Jack's words.

"You compared us? What we shared?" Cal asked, disbelief in his voice.

Tears sprung to my eyes, and I tried to gain footing on what was happening. It'd made sense at the time. Loving them was pulling me apart, and I was just trying to hold on. To deny the truth that was crashing through me right now.

"I couldn't choose," I whispered again. "I didn't know what to do."

"Quit fucking with me," Jack rasped. "Quit fucking with us." He glanced at Cal, then back at me. "Choose now, or walk away."

Boom. Shot to the heart.

The tears that teetered along my lower lashes spilled over. They thought I was playing them. The thoughts I'd written down were never meant to be a bad thing. I wanted clarity. But it didn't matter, because Jack wasn't entirely wrong. I'd listed everything. Compared. And watching his chest move on a ragged breath, I realized that I'd known the answer the whole time . . .

"I'm walking away," I whispered.

Jack's brows sliced down. Cal's body shot to stone that put a statue to shame. Both their searing gazes bit through my skin.

This had been inevitable. I'd known it. But I'd never prepared myself for actually having to walk away. For leaving them. Or for them letting me leave.

Jack didn't say a word, he just turned and walked out. My tears fell harder. We were over. Honest to God, totally over.

I took a step toward Cal, but he backed away. Those tears streamed faster. Because I looked down to find my hand reached out to him. He didn't reach back.

So much anguish showed behind his eyes, but he said nothing, just left the room.

It was cold. So painfully cold that my bones snapped like brittle wire. There was more than enough blame to go around. But the fact remained that whether it was now, or later, the choice between Jack and Cal would never be made. Not by me. Not ever.

All I could do was let the pain in, let it break me up and beat me down until it hurt so bad I was oblivious to the wound. Old wounds that hadn't healed, may never heal, cut wide open and seared from my chest to my shins.

Through foggy eyes and shaking steps, I made my way to the bedside table and grabbed my cell phone. It was a new year . . . but the promise of everything was gone.

I dialed Harper and tried to choke back the violent sobs of depression.

But it was useless.

Chapter 21

Opening my eyes had never hurt so badly. They were swollen from crying. My neck hurt like I'd been sleeping on a two by four. I tossed in the sheets and felt a warm hand smooth over my foot.

I shot up, thinking it was Jack or Cal.

"Good morning," Harper said, sitting at the end of the couch. She propped my feet in her lap with one hand and held a cup of coffee in the other.

The events from last night settled in to my brain. I was at Harper's house, well, Rhett's.

"Thanks for coming to get me last night." I glanced around. "Is Rhett back? I don't want to take up your couch." Also, I didn't want to see him, or anyone from the fire department.

"No, he's at the station until tomorrow."

I nodded and sat up. Harper handed me the cup of coffee. Cradling it in both palms, I let the mug warm my hands and tried not to think of today. The first day of the new year and already it was disaster.

"Do you want to talk about it?" she nudged.

"Not much to really say ... I lost them." I took a quick sip of coffee before the tears started again.

"It was a hard decision . . . the place they put you in from the beginning."

Yet, somehow, that didn't make it better. Yes, everything that was happening started from their plan. But that plan had been the sole reason I was the person I was. Both of them helped me. Loved me. And I walked out.

"I can't choose."

Those three words were fast becoming my mantra, and one I'd live the rest of my life hating.

Harper shook her head. "That's not true," she whispered. "You made a choice. You chose neither of them."

I squeezed my eyes shut. "It feels like the wrong choice."

Because my whole body hurt from needing them. The look in Jack's eyes and the sadness on Cal's face were all I could think about.

"In time, it will get easier." Though Harper was trying to make me feel better, I didn't think this would ever get easier. I loved them both with everything I was. And I walked. The question I'd been so mad about hit me hard.

How do you walk away from someone you love?

Jack had done it to me and I didn't understand. Now, it made more sense. He did it because he couldn't change the fact that the timing was off. He walked to give me space. To give himself space. To give Cal a chance. And, without Cal, I knew deep down a part of me would still be broken. It was the same logic that had made Cal keep the secret from me. The arrangement was a means to an end. An end I'd just enacted. And now, they weren't there. Cal didn't run after me, and Jack didn't open his arms to let me hide in them.

They let me go.

"Maybe focusing on something else will be good," she said.

209

"You have the key, right? We still going to the bank tomorrow?"

I nodded and swiped a hand over my eyes. "Yes. First thing. I want to know what's in there before the business meeting Anita has lined up tomorrow afternoon."

Harper nodded. "Do you really think this will make everything go away?"

I scoffed. "I have no idea. I don't know what my dad left. I don't even know if selling the company will make the harassment stop. I hope so. It stands to reason it will." Maybe I just needed something to believe in. An honest to God fresh start. But, no matter what happened, I also needed to stay away from the people I cared about until everything was solved.

"Thank you for taking me in last night, Harp. I'll be out of here tomorrow."

"You can stay as long as you need."

"Thanks, but I'll be fine. We get our insurance money tomorrow. I'll stay in a hotel until I find a place."

She went to argue, but I just smiled and stopped her. "I promise I can handle myself." I also didn't want to be too close to her. Yes, I knew Brock clearly hated me and had no problem hurting me. But, I had done all I could do. I just had to wait for my day in court.

Maybe with the company being sold and my father laid to rest, the truth would reveal itself and I could live in peace. Lonely and in peace.

"Sounds like we have a busy day tomorrow," Harper winked. "We?"

"You don't think I'd let you do all this alone do you? Hell no, I want to see what's in that box too. Maybe it's pirate treasure."

I laughed. "My dad wasn't really the pirate type."

"Still, I have a feeling, whatever it is, it's going to be a game changer."

"Or it could be a stamp collection."

"Looks like we'll know soon enough."

With that, I drank my coffee and thought about how not to cry for the next twenty-four hours until I finally put one mystery to rest.

Chapter 22

"This is it," Harper said, bouncing a little in her shoes.

I held the key to the bank lockbox and looked at the old hunk of metal on the table.

"I'll give you some privacy," the older gentleman banker said. As he walked out of the room, his footsteps echoed. The whole room was lined with lockboxes, neatly ordered and shelved. It was old and dingy. But in that small room, smelling mothballs and cold metal, was the first time I'd felt close to my father in a long time. Whatever was in there, it was a step to realizing that he was truly gone. And I wasn't sure how to deal with that.

"Are you going to open it?" Harper asked.

I nodded, words seeming to fade in the back of my throat before I could even speak them.

I put the small key in the lock and twisted. The snap of the lock gave way and I opened the long top.

"Paper," I said, examining a stack of folded forms.

Harper looked in. "That's it? Paper?"

I reached for the documents and opened them. The paper

whined like it hadn't been opened in years. It was stiff, and as I read the first page, my eyes got wider.

"This can't be . . . right. Can it?" I glanced from the forms to Harper, then back. I looked at the second page. Then the third. Harper came to stand behind me to read over my shoulder.

"Holy shit," she breathed. I could feel her eyes working a mile a minute, just like mine were, reading frantically. "Do you know what this means?"

I shook my head, then nodded, then shook.

"I think it means . . . " I flipped to the next page, "That my father's company is . . . mine."

"Look at this," Harper pointed at the date. "These are corporate documents that were drawn up right when your dad's business partnered with Anita."

"But, they didn't partner," I said, reading more. "This states that Anita put up money as a loan. She's not a partner. She's a creditor. She holds no stake in the company."

"So, why is she selling it?"

"My father was going to sell it. And when he did, Anita would be entitled to her initial funds, plus fifteen percent interest." I flipped another page. "But that's it."

"Wait," Harper said and turned back over the last page. "So, this says," she tapped on the paper, "That Anita only put up fifty grand. But the company is worth . . . "

I shrugged and did some mental math. "Probably closer to fifty million."

"Holy fucking ass and pandas!" Harper blew out a breath. "And that money goes to you." She ran her hand over the line that there, in black and white, stated me as the owner. "He put founding stock in your name years ago."

I looked to where Harper was pointing.

213

"Oh, my God, he did."

"That's a pretty big motive for the VanBurens to pull the shit they've pulled."

"Motive." The single word clicked everything together. It was what the detective was looking for. The link that tied this all together. Jack had been right. Why would someone – aka Brock – be after me if there was nothing to gain? "This is what Brock was looking for when he broke into my house."

"And when he didn't find it, it's probably why he burned the place."

"It couldn't have been him. He was in jail."

"Then it was your bitch of a step-mother."

I nodded. "That makes sense."

Harper just shook her head. "If you're not in his will, and there isn't any other documentation on this, then once the company is sold, these documents won't matter. Lana, you have to get to that meeting. Because this is the only way to show that when the company sells, the money goes to you."

I nodded. The meeting was set for later today, so I had a few hours, but this was ... terrifying. It all made sense now.

"This was why the stalking started in the first place," I muttered. "I think my father wanted to sell months ago, that's why Brock came back. Anita must have found out. He could have left her and taken his money with him. I think my dad was going to walk away from Anita and take the profits of the business with him."

"That makes sense," Harper agreed. "Maybe they found out somehow about the documents and killed him when he wouldn't—"

Harper stopped when my retch knocked on my throat.

"I'm sorry," she whispered. "I didn't mean to be insensitive."

214

"You're not," I said. "Aside from everything, my father and I had a flawed relationship." I thought back to all the bad moments. All the times I needed him and he wasn't there. Then I thought of the few things he'd said. The hope I'd held on to. "He told me to stay away from Brock," I whispered. Maybe, somehow, he was trying to warn me. Maybe I was grasping at something that could never be. But I honestly didn't think so. Somewhere, deep down, I had to believe my father loved me. In his own way, maybe he even tried to warn me.

"So, you think they had something to do with his death?"

"Yes," I said, without hesitation. My father died in the early afternoon before my house burned. Which meant that it could have been either Brock or Anita. I gripped the papers tighter. "Now, it's time to prove it." Because, like Harper said, this is one hell of a motive and enough to at least haul both of their VanBuren asses in for questioning again.

"I'll bring the car around back," Harper said and rushed out. I stood for a moment, looking at the papers and not caring about the money. What struck me was that my father cared. On some level, he'd thought of me. And it was the last sliver of goodness and despair that coursed through my veins. I wouldn't let Brock or Anita get away with hurting another Case. I wouldn't let them take everything my father built for themselves while torturing me the whole time.

This ended now.

Chapter 23

Shoving the documents into the front of my jacket, I hugged them close and stood on my toes, looking down the alley. No sign of Harper yet. We'd parked a bazillion miles away this morning, since there'd been no spots nearby.

The sky was graying with a snow cloud moving in front of the sun. The alley was bleak and dark, and there was a good reason I hated this side of the city. I wanted to call Jack and tell him everything. Wanted to hug Cal and listen to him reassure me.

I could do neither.

I was alone. Standing in the cold with the memory of my father and, hopefully, the end to the VanBurens in my life.

"Did you have an eventful trip?" a nasty feminine voice rang out.

"Anita?"

She rounded the corner and walked toward me, her black designer trench coat tied around her waist and her heels clicking on the pavement. I'd never seen a more evil look in anyone's eye. But I wasn't backing down. Not now. Not ever again.

"You disgust me," I told her, and held tight to the papers

216

under my jacket. "You killed my father, didn't you? And for what? Money?"

She scoffed. "A *lot* of money." She took another step. "And no, I didn't kill him." The way she smiled after saying that left little faith in her words. "But, you're going to hand me those papers right now."

She looked at where I was concealing them, then at my face. How the hell could she have known? Unless . . .

"You've been following me?"

She lifted a shoulder with a shrug. "You're not hard to keep tabs on, Lana. But you should have stayed in that cabin and let this play out instead of making a mess of things."

My eyes shot wide. She'd known I was at Jack and Cal's cabin the whole time.

"That was your grand plan? Keep me out of the picture until you sold the business and collected the money?"

"You've always been a nuisance."

"You didn't have to kill my dad!" I yelled at her. She took another step and pulled a small pistol out of her large coat pocket. My palms went sweaty at the same time my blood froze. We were in a back alley, but surely someone around the front would hear a gun go off. I wasn't in the best frame of mind to think of logistics now, though. All I saw was the barrel of the weapon and my heart dropped.

Did my father stare down the same gun?

I let what little anger I had beat out the fear. It was time for logic.

"You really think shooting me, where everyone can hear, is going to help your cause?"

"Everyone? There's barely a few strangers around the front of the building. I'll be gone by the time anyone comes to find you.

Now, give me the papers. Don't think for a moment I won't pull the trigger."

I believed her. But, no, I wouldn't stand down.

"I'm going to the police. And you won't touch my father's company or get a dime from it." I lifted my chin. "You don't scare me." And for the first time in a long time, it was true.

"Stupid girl."

She lunged at me, her free hand shoving at my stomach to get to the papers I was hiding. I kicked out and shoved her away with my free hand. She wobbled back, her heels scraping the wet concrete, but righted herself quickly. She was back on me, the cold gun pressing into my chest. It was heavy enough that I felt the ridges of the barrel abrade my skin.

A clicking sound ... like the cocking of a gun, shot a fresh dose of fear through my system. She was ready to kill me for the papers. For the money. I didn't have to see her finger on the trigger to know it was there.

But I was fighting for something bigger than her reasons. I was fighting for my dad. And for myself. For all the lies and the evil they rained down on everyone they encountered. Brock hurt people. Anita hurt people. I wouldn't go down without a fight.

I would never slink away from them again.

I went to knock her away—

Bang!

The gun went off and it was so loud that it hurt my ears. But it was nothing compared to the pain that exploded through my body. A concentrated prick of heat ripped open my skin and trickled through my body like an icicle melting slowly.

I kicked at Anita and she fell back, the gun sliding away with a loud scratching noise.

She stood and bounded toward me. I was weak. Numb. A

cold blast of air hit and instantly chilled my bones. She was coming for me, and I couldn't raise my arm to ward her off.

Fight! I had to fight. I tried to move, but my legs locked, then softened against my commands. I slumped to my knees.

Why was I so cold?

So weak?

I saw her eyes lock on mine. Five steps away … arms outstretched. She was going to take the papers. Take everything. And I couldn't stop her.

A screeching noise and skidding tires echoed over the low hum in my ears. A red car slammed into Anita and sent her flying back against the brick wall.

Harper.

I looked at my friend. She was moving so fast. Rounding the front of the car and coming right at me.

"Lana!" She knelt in front of me. "Oh, God, Lana, I'm going to get you help, okay? Just hang on." She yanked her cell phone from her pocket and dialed frantically.

"Hang on?" I asked. Why was Harper so scared? So worried? She'd saved me from Anita. She'd hit her with her car.

I looked at Harper's face. Her big eyes were teary. I wanted to tell her it was okay. She saved me from Anita. It was self-defense. She wouldn't be in trouble.

I stepped toward her, but my leg wouldn't move … because I was kneeling on them. When had that happened? I thought I remembered slumping down. Maybe I didn't? I tried to replay the scuffle, but came up short.

Another blast of cold shot through my body. Snowflakes started to fall, that heavy cloud in the sky rising higher. I thought of Jack's dark eyes. The way he held me. How he made me feel strong and weak at the same time.

Another snowflake fell.

I thought of Cal. How he made everything better. Made me laugh. Made me hope.

I loved them.

I watched another fluff of snow land on my shoulder and looked to find ... red.

It was all over my jacket.

I went to touch it and realized I couldn't move. Couldn't think. A searing edge of pain sliced through my chest and down my arm, and it hurt so bad. As if whatever numbing agent I'd been coasting on had worn off.

I was lying on the ground. When had I laid down?

"I'm tired ... " I said to Harper. "And cold."

"I know, honey, I know," she said, crying and tugging her jacket off to press it against the red spot, all while balancing the phone between her shoulder and ear. I didn't know what she was saying. But she looked so upset.

She pushed her jacket hard against me.

"Ah!" I screamed. "That hurts. Please stop."

"I know. I'm so sorry. But help is on the way. Just hang on."

I heard sirens in the background and thought of Cal. Was he coming? Coming after me? A small smile hit my face.

"He's coming for me," I whispered.

With that, I closed my eyes, and let the happy thought take me down.

Chapter 24

A flash of bright light hit my eyes. The harsh noise of metal clacking together snapped against my eardrums. Voices. So many voices. But I couldn't see anything. Couldn't feel anything except a large mask covering my nose and mouth.

I needed air. Badly. But it wasn't coming.

I was lying flat.

I tried to move, but couldn't.

The coolness crept in so potent it permeated my bones.

I wanted to touch my chest. Pound on it. Anything if it would just let me breathe . . .

"Get her up there. On my count. One, two, lift!"

A loud boom and my body jostled. I didn't recognize the voice. But a beeping sound got louder and louder. The voices kept talking in a way I didn't understand.

"I've got absent lung sounds on the right."

Pressure poked different spots on my chest. I tried to beg to these far off voices for help. But I couldn't even exhale enough to whisper.

"Have the one-way valve ready," that same voice said.

A slice of agony burst through my ribs and a rush of blessed air released. I blinked as fast as I could, but it didn't help. Just flecks of light pierced the darkness.

A loud bang rang out. Like a fist against solid glass. "God damn it!"

That voice I recognized. It was Cal.

"Cal!" I screamed out for him. But my mouth didn't move. I could have sworn I screamed. Another bang. Finally, a little clarity struggled into my vision. Hands flew above my face, passing medical instruments back and forth.

Hospital. I was in the hospital.

A memory tapped on my skull briefly. I remembered Anita . . . the gun . . . the pain.

Forcing my gaze as far as it could go, I finally saw him. Saw my Cal. He was on the other side of a window. Banging at it.

I couldn't move. I just looked at Cal. He was so mad. So scared. His big fists resting against the window as he looked in. Looked at me.

When his blue gaze met mine, his massive chest stumbled on a heavy breath, and so much water lined his eyes that I could see it from the several feet and through the wall of glass that separated us.

He was beautiful. Like a phantom sent to watch over me. I didn't want him to be sad. I didn't want him to hurt.

He looked at me, his mouth moving, but I couldn't hear the words.

A flare of black eyes caught my attention. Jack. He was right next to Cal. He moved into my line of vision like a sleek angel of darkness. Only what I saw made my chest hurt. Which was odd, since I was numb. But this pain came from the inside.

Jack was deadly with his stare, but I'd never seen a look like this on his face before. Defeat. He looked lost. His thick lashes blinked once and rained tears with the action. Silent. Still. With a continuous stream of water falling from his eyes. He didn't move. Didn't speak. Just looked at me.

"Don't be sad," I tried to say. "Please . . . " I couldn't bear the look on his face. Couldn't bear it on Cal's. We were separated by a window and it seemed so trivial. It was so easy when life was stripped away and left nothing but the people you loved . . . who loved you back.

My eyes felt heavy. The low hum of all the voices faded together and a fog settled over my vision. I just needed to close my eyes . . . just for a moment.

"Her pressure is dropping!"

The last thing I saw was pure fear streak across Jack's face and Cal pounding the window, calling my name.

Chapter 25

Soft cool hands cupped my face. The smell of sugar cookies engulfed me, and I took a deep inhale.

"Bea?" I whispered, surprised to find my throat nearly closed up and scratchy.

"Yes, sweetheart. It's Aunt Bea. Open your eyes for me, sweet girl."

I tried. But they felt so heavy. So, I tried again. It took several seconds, but Bea's plump face finally came into focus, and it was a wonderful sight.

"Are you okay?" I asked.

She frowned. "You're asking if I'm okay?" She smiled. "You're the one who got shot."

Oh right . . . the pain in my chest and shoulder throbbed and reminded me quickly what had happened. I didn't want Bea to be around me if it wasn't safe.

"Anita and Brock . . . they are bad. They . . . "

"I know, honey. We called the police. Harper is still out there talking with them. They have an officer with Anita now. Your friend Harper broke Anita's leg and gave her a nasty concussion from hitting her with that car. Though I wish she would have reversed and driven over that horrible woman again," Bea grumbled.

I smiled. "It's really over?"

She nodded. "Yeah, honey."

"But, my dad. The company."

"They took Brock into custody regarding your dad. They have evidence he was the one who . . . " Bea glanced away, and I knew what she meant. Brock had pulled the trigger and killed my father. But they had him. He'd be punished. "Anita set the fire. They found all kinds of nasty stuff in her garage, and they are also charging her with a whole bunch of other things, including hurting you." She rubbed my face. "It's all over. They got them. You're safe now."

I closed my eyes and leaned into Bea's soft touch. Her thumbs brushed my cheeks as she held my face. It was soothing. Felt like . . . family.

When I opened them again, I noticed the small room was empty. My heart sank. Had I imagined Jack and Cal at the window?

"They're here," Bea said, as if reading my mind. But, however she knew my thoughts, I didn't care. "We got word you were in recovery and just one person could come back. I told them I was your aunt and got to come first." She winked. But there was a sadness to her expression. "The boys are walking holes in the floor out there. They didn't know if you'd want to see them . . . "

My heart broke. No matter what, I'd never not want to see them.

"I want to see them. Very much."

Bea nodded, just as Jack's menacing voice sounded from down the hallway. Saying something along the lines of, "try and stop me from seeing her."

I laughed and Bea rolled her eyes.

"It seems that they are on their way."

That was just like them. Pushing in when there was no other way. And I loved them for it.

When Jack bounded through the door and I saw him, a smile so wide split my cheeks that it actually hurt. The nurse was telling him to leave.

"It's okay," I managed. Then Cal was right behind him, shoving his way through the door. "They can stay."

The nurse eyed them, then left. Bea patted my cheek, "I'll just go get some Jell-O."

She left, leaving me with a very tired, very annoyed looking Jack and a very pissed off Cal.

"Jesus, baby," Jack whispered and hovered near me, afraid to touch me. "I'm so sorry."

"I can't believe we almost lost you," Cal said, and came to the other side of the bed and held my hand. "I'm sorry too. For everything."

"There's nothing to be sorry about," I said. Jack ran the back of his finger along my cheek. He looked ready to tear at the seams from exhaustion.

"There's much to be sorry about," he said. "We let you walk away. I was trying to control a situation that wasn't mine to control. I shouldn't have forced your hand."

"I walked away, and I'll never forgive myself for that," I said.

"We messed up," Cal said. "From the beginning. But if you'll have us, we'll make it right. Every day."

"Us?" I asked. Cal squeezed my hand and shot a look to Jack.

"Yes, *us*. We won't make you choose. We'll be whatever you need us to be. Just as long as it's forever."

My heart hurt with so much hope it was ready to burst open. But logistics crept in.

"How can that work? I will never be able to choose. And a relationship between me and both of you is not . . ."

"Standard?" Jack finished.

I nodded.

"I don't give a fuck about what everyone else thinks. Nothing about any of this has been standard from the beginning. You make my life worth a damn," Jack said. "I won't give you up, you understand?"

I smiled. "Even if it means you'll have to share?"

He nodded and looked at Cal. "There's no other man I trust more than you."

Cal squeezed my hand. "I'm not letting you get away. Ever. Jack and I will do whatever it takes to keep you. Whether you like it or not."

"Promise?" I asked, with a sob coming through. Because they were family. My family.

"Yeah, Kitten, we promise." Cal rose and kissed me softly on the lips. As soon as he pulled back, Jack stood and leaned down to kiss me.

Could this really work? Maybe it was the drugs talking, but I seriously thought, why not? When death was on the table and life was short, clarity in the small things seemed so . . . clear. I loved them. Wanted to be with them. And we could.

The rest be damned.

"Okay," the doctor said, shuffling in, a white coat gliding around his frame while he looked at his clipboard. "I'm happy to say everything looks good. You should make a full recovery. Surgery went well. The bullet is out and . . ." he read over the form then looked up at Jack. Then glanced at Cal. "Which one of you is the husband?"

"Husband?" I asked.

"Yes," the doctor said, now doing a double-take between Cal and Jack. "Oh, fiancé?" he tried again. "Next of kin," he finally settled on, but I still had no answer for any of those inquiries.

I just sat there in shock. This was how it would always be. Unsure how to answer that kind of question.

"We're both her next of kin," Jack said. Cal nodded in agreement, and the doctor didn't push.

I smiled at my men. My men. That would take some getting used to. But they were trying. Maybe we really could figure out the rest later.

The doctor nodded. "Well, I'm happy to say that a full recovery is expected."

Cal smiled bigger than I'd ever seen and Jack was beaming ear to ear.

Relief and happiness swept over the room. They both loved me. And I was the luckiest girl in the entire universe for that fact.

"I'll give you all a moment. Buzz the nurse if you need anything," the doctor said, and left.

Jack ran two hands through his hair and smiled up at the ceiling. "I can't believe you're really okay," he whispered, like the last of his fear was let go.

"There's so much to figure out," I whispered.

Jack strummed his thumb along my cheekbone. "And we will," he said. "We're in this together."

"We're family," Cal said, and took the thoughts out of my mind. Family. Our own family.

Could this really work? It had to. Because I was fighting for all of us now. And judging by the look on Cal and Jack's faces, so were they.

"The real world doesn't work like this," I said.

"I don't give a shit," Cal responded. "There's no law that says you can't keep two guys on your roster."

I laughed, Cal always made things seem so easy. But I had been thinking marriage, and that wasn't something that was possible. Not to both of them.

The hand on my face brushed again, lightly along my jaw this time. "We will figure it out. We understand you won't choose. It won't change that we're both here for you. We aren't going anywhere. We'll make it work."

"I love you," I whispered. I looked into Jack's dark eyes and felt like I'd come home. Then I looked at Cal and knew I was whole.

One night had spurred a total sense of completeness.

I was theirs.

And they were mine.

Forever.

Epilogue

One Year Later . . .

"We've got to tell Bea to stop spoiling her," Cal said, putting another wrapped box under the Christmas tree.

"She just loves her great niece," I said, rocking my daughter to sleep. Tomorrow was Christmas. The past year had slowed down and been wonderful. Anita and Brock were in prison for their crimes. Harper was pregnant, and I was back at the cabin that was my saving grace with two men I loved.

"How's my angel?" Cal said, coming over to us and gently running a palm over his daughter's light blonde hair. She opened her eyes.

"Say, 'Daddy is keeping me awake'," I said in a cooing voice and Cal smiled at me.

"She's just so . . . perfect."

I nodded. She really was.

Jack walked in with hot chocolate, placed the mugs on the coffee table, and sat next to me on the couch.

"There's my girls," he said, and leaned in to run a finger along his daughter's chubby cheek. Her dark eyes blinked a few times and she looked at Jack.

We didn't know who the biological father was, because it didn't matter. They both were daddies. It had been the best year of my life. I'd taken over my father's company, and brought it back from the brink. What once was Case-VanBuren was now CPM Investments. While a part of me would always be Lana Case, I was a part of the Powell-Malone family.

My family. Our family.

"Have you thought more about our offer?" Jack asked.

I looked at him. Then at Cal.

"You mean marriage?"

"Yes," Jack said.

I shook my head. "You know I'll never choose."

Cal grinned. "It wouldn't be anything except a legal technicality."

"Still can't choose," I said.

Cal blew out a breath. "You know she's stubborn."

"Believe me, I know," Jack grumbled.

"Looks like we'll just have to choose for her," Cal said with a wink.

"Good luck with that," I responded. "I think our own personal commitment ceremony sounds better. Something just for us."

"I like that," Jack said. "It will go well with these." Jack and Cal each pulled a ring from their pocket. Jack had a single band with black diamonds and Cal had one with blue diamonds.

"Oh, my God, they're beautiful," I said, and tears lined my eyes.

"However we need to do it, just realize you're ours. Forever."

I smiled and they put the rings on my finger.

"Wow . . ." Another tear fell, but I was so happy I couldn't hide it. "This is a pretty wonderful Christmas present," I said, then looked at Jack then Cal. "To think I was just going to tell you I was pregnant again."

Both of their faces lit up.

"Are you serious?" Cal said.

I nodded. "You two won't leave me alone, is it any wonder?"

"There's my sassy girl," Jack said. And kissed me hard. "God, I love you."

"I love you too."

Cal leaned down and kissed my lips, my nose, and my cheek until I laughed. "Love you so much, Kitten."

"I love you too."

And I did. Holding my world in my arms and surrounded by the men that gave me a future, I truly was happy.

Acknowledgments

Thank you Anna, Grace, Tara, Clara, and the amazing team for all your hard work on this book. Thank you Jill Marsal for being the best agent in the galaxy. Thank you E-book formatting fairies for the wonderful edits. Thank you to my incredible family and friends for supporting me. Special thanks to Cary and Brittany for all your support. You both are made of pure awesome!